Annie

Mary Christner Borntrager

HERALD PRESS
Scottdale, Pennsylvania
Waterloo, Ontario

Library of Congress Cataloging-in-Publication Data
Borntrager, Mary Christner, 1921-
          Annie / Mary Christner Borntrager.
            p. cm. — (Ellie's people)
          ISBN 0-8361-9070-X (alk. paper)
          ISBN 0-8361-9071-8 (large-print pbk.)
          1. Amish—United States—Fiction. I. Title. II. Series:
Borntrager, Mary Christner, 1921- Ellie's people.
PS3552.07544A85 1997
813'.54   dc21   96-50126

The paper used in this publication is recycled and meets the mini-
mum requirements of American National Standard for Informa-
tion Sciences—Permanence of Paper for Printed Library Materials,
ANSI Z39.48-1984.

This is a work of fiction but true to Amish life. Scripture is freely
adapted from the King James Version of *The Holy Bible*.

*To Bethany,
Missy, and Rachel—
with love*

ELLIE'S PEOPLE

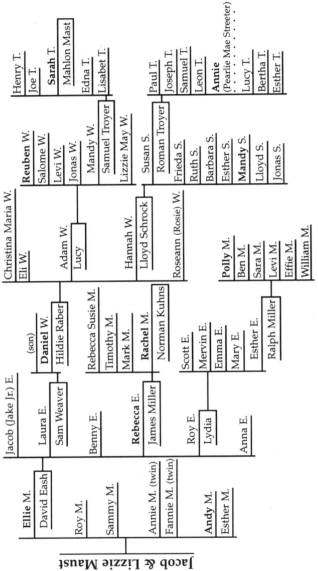

Jacob & Lizzie Maust

Jacob (Jake Jr.) E.
- Laura E. — Sam Weaver
- Benny E.
- **Rebecca** E. — James Miller
  - Roy E.
  - Lydia
  - Anna E.

Christina Maria W.
- Eli W.
- Adam W. — Lucy
  - **Daniel W.** — Hildie Raber
    - (son)
  - Rebecca Susie M.
  - Timothy M.
  - Mark M.
  - **Rachel M.** — Norman Kuhns
- Hannah W.
- Lloyd Schrock — Roseann (Rosie) W.
  - Scott E.
  - Mervin E.
  - Emma E.
  - Mary E.
  - Esther E. — Ralph Miller

Reuben W.
- Salome W.
- Levi W.
- Jonas W. — Samuel Troyer
  - Mandy W.
  - Lizzie May W.

Susan S. — Roman Troyer
- Frieda S.
- Ruth S.
- Barbara S.
- Esther S.
- **Mandy S.**
- Lloyd S.
- Jonas S.

- Henry T.
- Joe T.
- **Sarah** T. — Mahlon Mast
- Edna T.
- Lisabet T.

- Paul T.
- Joseph T.
- Samuel T.
- Leon T.
- **Annie** (Pearlie Mae Streeter) · · · · · · · ·
- Lucy T.
- Bertha T.
- Esther T.

Polly M.
- Ben M.
- Sara M.
- Levi M.
- Effie M.
- William M.

Ellie M. — David Eash
- Roy M.
- Sammy M.
- Annie M. (twin)
- Fannie M. (twin)
- **Andy M.**
- Esther M.

Contents

1
Different—But Friends

Lucy was excited. "Can she stay, Mom? Can she?"

"Hush once, Lucy," her mother admonished her. "You get too anxious. Run outside with Pearlie Mae and bring the clothes in from the line. Mrs. Streeter and I want to talk."

"I'll help you fetch them," Pearlie Mae offered.

Lucy didn't know what "fetch" meant. She had never heard it as an Amish word or as an English word. Nevertheless, she took the clothes basket and headed outdoors. Pearlie Mae followed.

The two girls were as different as night and day. Pearlie Mae had a deep dimple in each cheek and curly blonde hair. Her eyes were the blue of a bluebird's wings. When she smiled, her whole face lit up. An even set of sparkling white teeth and a sunny disposition added to her charm.

Lucy, however, was a plain, ordinary Amish child. This was nothing to be ashamed of. Her hair was straight and brown. She wore it pulled back in two tight braids, half hidden under a black cap. Deepset brown eyes gave her oval face a somber expression.

Lucy's one outstanding feature was a cute little nose. Too often she used that nose in expressing her pent-up feelings. If anything displeased her, she would stick that part of her face in the air and march off. Generally she was an obedient child.

"I can hardly reach the clothesline," laughed Lucy, grabbing at a shirt. The wind was blowing lustily.

"Here, I'll pull on one sleeve and you get the other one," Pearlie Mae suggested.

Both girls jumped to catch the garment but missed. They landed on the soft grass and giggled at their failed attempt.

Mrs. Streeter saw the girls' predicament as she was leaving. "Maybe it would help if you lowered the props."

She headed toward her car. "Now, Pearlie Mae, you be good while I'm gone. Come fetch your belongings and take them inside. Mrs. Troyer said you can bed with them till I get back. Be smart now, and mind!"

"When you aimin' to fetch me back, Maw?" Pearly Mae asked.

"Soon as I kin. It's a fur piece to see about your pappy."

The rattling car went chugging out the drive and on down the gravel road. Spirals of dust trailed behind. Soon the car and driver were lost to the view of the girls.

"Oh, I'm so glad you can stay," Lucy told Pearlie Mae.

"Me, too," her friend answered. "I like it here with you. Your Maw and Pappy don't feud, do they?" she asked.

Lucy didn't know what Pearlie Mae meant. How could she answer? "I don't think so," she said.

"Oh, you would know it if they feuded," Pearlie Mae told her.

"How would I know?"

"There'd be screaming and yelling and hitting. Sometimes they'd fling things at each other. One time Pappy flung a chair at Maw, and it hit me."

"Oh, no, my mom and dad would never do that!"

"I don't like it," Pearlie Mae told Lucy. "Pappy ain't come home fer nigh a week. Maw and Uncle Louie aim to find him."

"But why does she want him back if he's so mean?" Lucy wondered.

"He isn't mean when he's off the jug," Pearlie Mae said.

"Why do you talk so funny?" Lucy asked.

"I don't talk funny," Pearlie Mae defended herself.

"Girls," called Mrs. Troyer, "aren't you finished taking those clothes down? Hurry and bring them in. It is clouding up and looks like it might make down rain."

"Now who talks funny?" laughed Pearlie Mae.

Roman and Susan Troyer and seven children lived as next-door neighbors to the Streeters. Susan was one of Lloyd and Hanna Schrock's daughters. She belonged in the lineage of Ellie's People.

Like all their Amish relatives before them, they were respected and well-liked in the community. Always willing to lend a helping hand, Mrs. Troyer could hardly refuse when her neighbor asked to leave Pearlie Mae for a few days.

Lucy was almost eight years old and Pearlie Mae was already eight. Lucy had four brothers and two sisters. Pearlie Mae was an only child.

"My, you brought lots of stuff!" exclaimed Lucy. "How long can you stay?"

"Don't reckon I know. But I hope a long spell."

"I don't know what a spell is, but I hope real long." Then Lucy added, "We use a *Schpelle* (straight pins) to make our clothes fast."

"How do you fast clothes?" Pearlie Mae wondered.

"You do, that's all," Lucy answered.

"Lucy, fold the diapers and dampen down the clothes for ironing. You can't play just because Pearlie Mae is here."

Like all Amish, Lucy was taught to work.

"Want to help?" Lucy asked Pearlie Mae.

"Sure, if you show me how," Pearlie Mae said. "We're different, but we're friends anyway."

2
Almost Amish

Days turned into weeks, and still Mrs. Streeter had not returned. The Troyer's had no idea how to go about finding her. So Pearlie Mae stayed.

"Susan," Roman told his wife, "don't you think it's time to dress Pearlie Mae in our Amish way? I don't like taking her to church dressed so fancy."

"Ya, Roman, I had thought about that, too. Lucy has been asking why she can't have nice clothes like Pearlie Mae!"

"And that name!" exclaimed Roman. "It sure isn't for Amish."

"No, it isn't," agreed Susan, "but I'm afraid we can't do anything about that. She's eight years old and has always gone by that name."

"Couldn't we just call her 'Annie,' or some common Amish name, until her mother comes for her?" Roman suggested to his wife.

"I'll talk to her about it," she promised.

It would mean more sewing to outfit Pearlie Mae in the Amish way. Susan Troyer already had her hands full. She made almost all the clothes her family wore. With seven to sew for besides her husband and herself, it kept her busy.

The children ranged in ages from sixteen-year-old Paul to one-year-old Esther. Lucy was the oldest girl. Whenever their mother would have a new baby, one of Lucy's aunts came to help out.

Perhaps, thought Susan, *I can have Maut John's Viola come help during the summer.*

Viola had not married and had worked in various Amish homes.

"Lucy," Mother called. "Run upstairs and bring me your dark-blue Sunday dress. Bring your white organdy apron and your black cap, too."

This seemed like a strange request to Lucy, but she obeyed.

"Now, where is Pearlie Mae?" Mother asked.

"She is heeding the baby," Lucy answered.

"Go watch the baby and tell Pearlie Mae I want her."

Quickly Lucy ran and gave Pearlie Mae her mother's orders. "I'll stay here with the baby. You go on inside."

"What does your maw want me fer?" Pearlie Mae asked.

"I don't know," Lucy answered. "Just go once."

"Pearlie, I want to talk to you. We don't know why your mother hasn't come for you yet. I know you must miss her. Until she comes, Roman and I think it best to dress you Amish."

"You mean like Lucy?"

"Ya, like Lucy."

"Oh, I'd be pleasured to!" Pearlie answered.

"Come here, then, and try these on." Susan handed her Lucy's dress, apron, and cap. "Take them to the bedroom and change. When you come out, I'll button the dress for you."

Pearlie was so excited. She hurried so much that she put the dress on backward. That didn't look or feel right. She turned it around, slipped on the apron over top of the dress, and went to show Mrs. Troyer.

"What took you so long?" Susan asked.

"Oh, I got it wrong first. Can I keep it?"

"Well, let's see. It fits pretty good. A little short, but otherwise it's not bad."

"Oh, Mrs. Troyer, I like it, and I like living here with you until Maw comes. Can I keep these clothes? Can I? Just for a spell?"

"Yes, you can have this outfit. Roman says we should dress you Amish like Lucy. I'll make you a few new dresses and a couple for Lucy. My husband would like if we called you Annie. He says Pearlie is not an Amish name. Would you care if we did that?"

"I won't mind! I won't mind at all. It would be *larpin'* (wonderful). I'll have two names. While I live here, I'll be Annie. But when I go back home, I'll be Pearlie Mae. Can I go tell Lucy and show her my dress?"

"Ya, but you must come in and change into one of Lucy's everyday dresses then."

"You mean I get to dress like Lucy right off?" Pearlie asked. She almost danced for joy.

"The sooner the better, Pearl—I mean, Annie," Susan corrected herself.

Pearlie hurried out to the shade tree where Lucy sat with her baby sister.

"Look, Lucy!" she exclaimed. "See what your maw did? She said I can wear them until my maw fetches me. Don't you like it?"

Lucy was surprised but pleased. "Why, that looks like my blue Sunday dress. It is my dress, and you look almost Amish. I like it."

"Your maw said I can keep it. She's going to make me some new ones and some for you, too. And guess what else! They're giving me a new name because Pearlie is not Amish."

"A new name!" exclaimed Lucy.

"Yes, I'm Annie now. Isn't that larpin'?"

"But I'm afraid I'll forget," Lucy told her.

"Oh, I'll help you remember," her friend said. "Come on, I have to go change into everyday clothes."

As the girls went inside, Pearlie asked, "Aren't you glad I'm almost Amish?"

3
Two Names

Sunday couldn't come soon enough for Annie. She would get to show how they had changed her.

"*Ach* (oh) my!" exclaimed Susan Troyer. "Roman, what shall I do about Annie's hair? It's so short I can't braid it."

"Try to pin the hair back and keep it under her covering," he suggested.

"*Ich duh was ich kann* (I'll do what I can)," Susan promised.

She wondered, *Why, oh, why did Mrs. Streeter cut her daughter's hair in the first place?*

The Troyer family had to use two buggies for church. Paul, who was sixteen and *rumschpringing* (running around with the youth), had his own rig.

Annie and Lucy sat in the backseat. They shared that place with six-year-old Bertha. Samuel and Joseph had to stand in the back of the single buggy box. Mother said it *verrunselt* (wrinkled) up the girls' dresses too much to ride back there.

"Don't forget to call me Annie," Pearlie Mae reminded everyone.

"I'll try to remember," Lucy promised.

"It's fun to go to your church," Pearlie Mae said. "But why does it last setch a long spell?"

"Because the bishop wants to tell us what the Bible says. It's a big book, you know," Lucy said, feeling very smart.

"At our preachin' we used to clap our hands and shout. We had a meetin' house with a cracked bell. Sometimes if we had all-day meetin's, we took dinner on the ground.

"There was a pump and lots of trees. Maw would spread a blanket to sit on while we et. Pa wasn't much fer holdin' to church. He told Maw and me to go if'n it pleasured us. It surely pleasured Maw. She was the best amen-shouter at the meetin'. Why is everyone so quiet at your meetin's?" Pearlie Mae asked.

"Annie," Roman told her, "we believe in being quiet so we can hear what the preacher is saying. Our way is not to cause any disturbance, and I want you to sit still and listen."

"But I can't understand. We don't talk like you do."

"I know, Annie, but the more you listen, the sooner you'll learn."

"Oh, Lucy, can you tetch me to talk Amish?" Pearlie Mae asked.

"I'll try, Pearl—I mean Annie. See, I almost forgot and called you Pearlie again."

The two girls giggled at the mistake.

"To tell you the truth," Lucy confessed, "I can't understand much of what the preachers say. But I am learning. You don't speak English like we do. Some of your words sound funny. Maybe we could start all over, and I can help you with both."

"I kin so speak English!" Pearlie Mae defended herself. "Tell me one word I kin't say right."

Lucy took the challenge. "Just now you said 'kin' for 'can' and 'kin't' for 'can't.' It sounds different," Lucy said.

"In your talk, how do you say 'kin'—I mean 'can'?" Pearlie asked.

"Why, 'can' is *kann* and 'can't' is *kann net*."

"That sounds funny, too, but I'll try," Pearlie decided.

"Anyway, we both look alike today. Well, almost," Lucy commented. "At least our dresses do."

That made the two young girls happy.

Roman and Susan were conversing in their own Pennsylvania Dutch (German), and Pearlie Mae wondered what they were talking about.

"Lucy, what are your folks saying?"

"Oh, they're trying to decide if they want to stay for church lunch."

"I hope we will. I like to stay and play with you and your friends. That's the best part," Pearlie Mae informed her.

"We're almost there," Susan told the girls. "Now if you whisper as much as the last time, I'll have to separate you. Lucy, you bring the *Windelsackli* (diaper bag). Pearl—Annie, pull your cap forward. Ach my, your hair just won't stay flat."

Secretly, Lucy wished she had curls like Annie's.

Oh well, once she did her own hair, maybe she could wave them a little like Lillian Swartz and Rosa Kaufman. The older people of the church disapproved. Lucy thought these girls were absolutely beautiful.

To the delight of both girls, the Troyer's stayed for the after-service meal. What fun Lucy and Annie had! They played drop-the-handkerchief and watched babies while the mothers ate lunch.

"Oh, Pearlie Mae," exclaimed Dena Chupp, "I like you in that dress."

"So do I," remarked Christina Beachy.

Ella Maust and Mabel Yoder agreed.

"Are you going to be Amish?" Christina asked.

"Yes, and Lucy is going to tetch me to talk like you do. And guess what! I'm going to have something none of you do."

The girls wondered about this.

"I'll have two names," she informed them. "My English name is Pearlie Mae, but now my Amish name is Annie."

4
They Preferred a Bletching

Rain was coming down in sheets. It was Sunday and the Troyer family was invited to spend the day with Stephen Beachy and his family.

"Oh, Annie," Lucy remarked, "you're soaked. When you walk, I even hear water squishing in your shoes."

"Yours, too," laughed Annie. "We're both soaked. Let's take our shoes off and splash in the puddles."

"Ach, we shouldn't," Lucy said.

Generally the children wore shoes only in cold weather. They even went to school and church in their bare feet. This morning, however, the girls decided to wear shoes to avoid washing their feet before going to the Beachy's. Waiting for the rain to let up, they slipped out of their soggy shoes.

"I'm glad these chickens are fed now," Lucy told Annie.

"Let's wait here in the doorway. These hens make

so much noise. Do you think they're talking to each other?" Annie asked.

"Oh, you're funny," Lucy said. "Chickens can't talk. They aren't people."

"Lucy, how do you say 'chicken' in Amish?"

"We say *Hinkel*."

Annie tried it. *"Hingul?"* she said.

"No," Lucy corrected her. "It's *Hinkel*." Annie tried a few more times until she could imitate Lucy accurately.

"That's right," Lucy praised her. "You did it, Annie. You got it right. Look, it's almost stopped raining. You bring the water bucket, Annie, and I'll bring the mash pail."

Carrying a pail in one hand and their shoes in the other, the girls started for the house. Laughing and squealing, they stepped in every available puddle. Cool mud oozed between their toes. Over and over Annie chanted, *"Hinkel, Hinkel."*

Then the kitchen door opened and Mr. Troyer called out sternly, *"Maed, do drin schnell* (girls, in here immediately)!"

Lucy knew by the tone of his voice that he meant business. She began to run, and Annie followed.

"Leave your shoes in the entryway," Roman said. "Lucy, what's wrong with you? You know better than to wear your shoes this time of the year. And what took you so long feeding the chickens?"

"We were waiting for the rain to let up," Lucy answered, trembling.

"Then when it did, you *hawwe in all Loch rumgepuddelt* (splashed around in every hole) you saw.

Didn't you?" Roman asked.

Lucy didn't answer.

"Well," her Dad asked again, "didn't you?"

"Ya, Dad," Lucy answered quietly.

"You and Annie go and get cleaned up, then help Mom get breakfast on the table."

The girls hurried to obey. Lucy informed Annie that some form of punishment was surely coming.

"What will happen to us?" Annie asked.

"Probably a hard *Bletching*," Lucy answered.

"What's a *Bletching*, Lucy?"

"A spanking," she answered.

"Does he hit real hard?" Annie inquired.

"Hard enough. It makes me cry."

"We were just havin' fun. I can't see why that's so bad."

"Dad wants us to take care of our shoes. I only have one pair, you know. They have to last all year. I knew we were not to play in the puddles when Mom needed my help in the house. Oh, Annie, I wish we wouldn't have done it."

But they had, and now it was time to take the consequences. Roman was seated at the head of the table, waiting patiently. He entertained baby Esther until Susan and the girls finished serving up the food.

Lucy wished the *Bletching* were over with. She wasn't very hungry. The only solace she could find was the upcoming visit at the Stephen Beachy home. Christina Beachy was a good friend. They had a lot of fun together. Maybe she could handle the punishment better if she kept thinking about seeing Christina.

Father pushed his chair away from the table. Turning to Lucy, he said, "Because you and Annie poked around, we are late. Mother hardly has time to do the dishes and clean up the kitchen. We, *Mamm un ich* (Mother and I), decided we will go to Stephen's without you and Annie."

The girls were crestfallen. All week they had looked forward to this event. Now both had to miss it. Surely Roman Troyer didn't mean it. But he did.

"After you girls get the dishes done and the kitchen tidied up, you can spend some time cleaning your muddy shoes. I'll set out the linseed oil. When they're washed and wiped clean, rub them with oil. It's good for the leather—keeps it from drying out."

Annie felt like crying. Truly the girls preferred to receive a *Bletching* rather than to miss the visit and the fun with Christina. But that was that.

5
Money Doesn't Grow on Trees

"Why couldn't we go visitin' with your folks?" Annie asked. "We were only havin' fun. They didn't tell us not to wear shoes when we chore, or to stay out of the rain puddles."

Lucy wiped tears away as she spoke. "My dad told me often to wear my shoes only for school or church, and then only in cold weather."

"But why?" questioned Annie. "My Maw and Pappy let me wear shoes anytime."

"Well, Dad says shoes are expensive and *Geld waxet net uff Beem.*"

"What does that mean, Lucy?" Annie asked.

"Ach, I forgot—I've heard it so often in our language. It means money doesn't grow on trees."

"Is your Pappy poor?" Annie asked. "Your family doesn't seem poor. We have good food to eat. Sometimes when my Pappy was on the jug, Maw and I only had black-eyed peas and fatback."

Lucy had never heard of such food. She didn't think she would like it. "My parents are not poor. They just don't like to spend money."

"Oh, I'd like to do that fine," Annie remarked. "I would buy ever so many things. Let's pretend we're rich and say what we would buy."

"First we must clean up the kitchen and wash the milk pails and separator parts," Lucy reminded Annie.

Roman Troyer's did not ship milk on Sundays. During the week the truck picked up their milk and took it to the local cheese house. But on Sunday the milk was separated from the cream by their De Laval separator. They churned the good, rich cream into butter. The skim milk was divided between hogs, cats, and chickens.

"Can't we play first and then finish the work?" Annie asked.

Lucy's brother Paul heard that question. He was sixteen and no longer went visiting with his parents on the in-between Sundays, when church was not held in their district.

"*Nee*, Lucy, *tu dein Arewet schnell* (no, Lucy, do your work quickly)," he advised her. "You'll have more fun if your work is done."

Annie laughed. "You made a rhyme," she pointed out.

"I hadn't thought about that," he remarked. "It just happened."

Annie laughed again.

"Don't forget," Paul reminded the girls. "You're

supposed to clean your muddy shoes."

Lucy sulked at this. "He acts as if he's our boss. Just because Mom and Dad are gone, he tries to tell us what to do. I hope he goes to play ball this afternoon. Then we can do what we please. Come on, Annie, we might as well get it done."

"I know," Annie agreed. "Let's plan what we would buy while we work with the milk pails and things. You want to wash or dry?"

"I'll wash," Lucy said. She was not at all enthused with Annie's idea.

"You start," Annie offered the first turn to Lucy.

"Right off, I'd buy two pairs of shoes. Then if one pair got dirty, I'd have another one."

"Oh, Lucy, is that all? I'd buy a hundred pair. Then if they were dirty, I'd throw them away and buy others." She giggled to help cheer Lucy up. Soon the task in the milk house was finished.

As the girls went back to the house, they took a cool drink of water from the outdoor pump. A tin cup was shared by all who drank there. The girls took turns pumping and drinking until their thirst was quenched, then rinsed out the cup and hung it on the wire hook attached to the pump.

"Better get to those shoes now," Paul told them again. "Spread the newspaper on the floor good and thick. Be careful not to get oil on the floor. Here, use these." He handed each some old rags.

Lucy tilted her head, sticking that little nose in the air. Snatching the rag from her brother, she mumbled, "Boss, boss, boss."

"*Was saagst du* (what did you say)?" Paul asked.

"You're bossy," Lucy told him.

"Look here, young miss, I'm only helping you. If you played around all day and didn't do as you were told, what would happen? You know you'd be in for a good *Bletching.*

"I'm going over to Elam's this afternoon. Some of us are going to pitch horseshoes. If you get busy and clean those shoes without grumbling, I'll help you get dinner and give you each a piece of Juicy Fruit gum."

He did not need to say more. Juicy Fruit gum! That was almost as prized as a pair of new shoes. Paul kept it on hand to share with a girl he might take to Sunday evening singings.

Now Lucy was happy. Maybe her brother was not so bad after all. The lunch of cold fried chicken, applesauce, and half-moon pies was delicious. After Paul left, the girls did the dishes and continued their buying game. Although it spited Lucy that she missed visiting her friend Christina, she learned a lesson in obedience.

"Come here, girls," Roman said later that evening. "What you did was wrong. The Bible says, 'Children, obey your parents.' Lucy, you have been told not to wear those shoes for play, and"—Lucy knew what was coming—"*Geld waxet net uff Beem,* you know."

6
The Letter

"Look, Mom," Lucy said. "Here's a letter for you."

Seldom did Susan get a letter in the mail. Most of the news she gleaned from *The Budget.* This was a weekly newspaper with articles from Amish scattered throughout the United States and Canada.

"Now, who would be sending me a letter?" Susan wondered.

"I don't know," Lucy replied, "but here it is."

The envelope was smudged and gray. There was no return address. Carefully Susan removed its contents and began reading.

"Ach my, no!" she exclaimed, sinking into the nearest chair.

"Mom, *was is letz* (what's wrong)?" Lucy asked. "Who is the letter from?"

"Oh, Lucy, it's from Annie's Uncle Louie."

"What does it say?"

"I can't tell you right now," her mother answered.

"Where is Annie?"

"She was out in the backyard trying to catch a butterfly."

"Go get her. And then I want you two girls to clean upstairs," her mother instructed.

Cleaning upstairs meant shaking all the throw rugs, dusting, and sweeping.

"But Mom, this is Friday. We always do that on Saturday."

"Yes, I know, but this week we will be different."

Lucy couldn't understand, but she obeyed.

"Take your time and *butz* (clean) real good," Susan told them. This, too, was different. Generally the girls were told to hurry and not *schtooffel* (poke) around. "Take the yellow scrub bucket and wash the stair steps, but don't *puddle* (splash) and play.

"Something is wrong with Mom," Lucy confided in Annie. "She got a letter in today's mail, and it upset her when she read it."

"What did it say? Who was it from?" Annie asked.

"I forget who sent it, and she didn't tell me what it said."

"Oh, Lucy, can't you remember who it's from?"

"Well, I think it's from your uncle or someone like that."

"You must be mistaken. My uncle wouldn't know your mom. I hardly remember him myself. Anyway, you must be wrong."

But Lucy wasn't wrong. Mrs. Troyer read the short letter the second time. She was sure there must be a mistake. The words seemed to leap out at her with frightening news. Her mind was in a whirl.

Baby Esther began to cry as she tipped over in her walker. This brought Susan back to reality. She must take care of her bawling baby. The letter would just have to wait. It was a serious matter which she and Roman needed to discuss.

She picked up the baby and checked the bump on her forehead. "Now, now," Susan comforted the frightened child. "I'll put a little butter on that ouchie. You're more scared than hurt."

Soon Esther quieted down and contentedly ate the crackers her mother offered her.

Even as she tended to her little one's needs, Susan's mind was on that letter. What would Roman say? What should they do? It was only early afternoon. Roman and the boys would not be home before chore time. The matter would just have to wait until the children were all in bed. This was something not to be discussed in their presence.

Mechanically Susan went about her household duties. The kitchen cupboards needed cleaning, and several pairs of the boys' pants needed mending. She wanted to finish varnishing the china cabinet. The boys had been begging for some chicken and dumplings, so she promised them they would have some for supper.

Susan worked on the cupboards, washing each shelf and neatly replacing the dishes. Next she finished the varnish job. Soon Esther started to fuss, so Susan changed her, filled her bottle, and put her in her crib. Picking up a pair of trousers, she sat down in the hickory rocker for a brief rest while mending.

She was far too fidgety for sit-down work. Making

sure the baby had gone to sleep, Susan went to catch a chicken for that evening's meal. She had to remain active. As she worked, she was silently praying.

"Oh, Lord, what would you have us to do about the terrible news we got today? Show us the way. We must tell the bishop about this."

It did not take Susan long to dress out a nice, fat hen. She had done it many times. Since the boys were older, they could do it for her. She had meant to ask Paul to do it, but somehow it had slipped her mind. Now she was glad she could get out of the kitchen for a bit.

As she returned to the house, she heard Lucy say, "We're all done. Now I'm going to ask Mom about the letter."

To avoid her daughter's question, Susan quickly sent the girls to sweep the porch and walks. The afternoon just seemed to drag by.

7

Our Secret

Lucy was not one to give up easily once her curiosity was aroused. She kept begging to know about the mysterious letter.

"Lucy, I don't want you to bother me anymore about that letter," her mother said. "If I wanted to tell you, I would have done so. Some things are not for children to know. At least not until I talk to Dad about it."

I'll find out, Lucy determined to herself.

"Something in that letter upset my Mother," she confided to Annie, "and I'm going to find out what it was."

"How are you going to do that?" Annie asked.

"Don't worry, I'll find a way," Lucy assured her.

Annie had no doubt that she would. *Perhaps,* Annie thought, *it might be better if Lucy didn't find out.*

"Something troubling you, Susan?" Roman asked his wife. She had forgotten to put the chicken and dumplings on the table. The baby's high-chair tray was not in place. Susan hadn't spoken a word since the men came in for supper.

"I wonder if this is all we're getting to eat," Paul teased. "Only bread and water after a hard day's work?"

"Ach my," Susan exclaimed, hurrying to bring the food to the table. "What was I thinking?"

"That's what we'd like to know," fourteen-year-old Joseph said.

"All right, boys," Roman chided, noticing Susan's trembling hands and sober expression. Generally she would laugh along with the family, but not this time. "Let's settle down and eat. If Mom wants to tell us, she will," Roman told them.

"We'll talk about it later, Roman," Susan said.

She wanted to tell him she received a letter which he needed to see. Her voice began to break, and she didn't trust herself to say more. Most of the meal was eaten in strained silence.

Leon, eleven, and Bertha, six, began some childish bickering, but Roman quieted them. Annie, Samuel, and Joseph all complimented their mom on how good the supper was. They were sincere, and it truly was delicious. They thought that would lift their mom's spirits, but she was still preoccupied with something.

Lucy silently agreed that it was a good meal. However, her mind was busy working out a plan.

Before leaving the table, Roman told Paul to put Star in the box stall for the night. "I believe she may have her colt before morning."

Star was one of their best driving horses. This news

brought excitement to the children.

"Oh, goody, a new *Hutschli* (colt)," Leon exclaimed.

"I hope she'll have a filly," Joseph remarked. "I'd like to have it for my buggy horse when I turn sixteen."

"You have to get a buggy first," Samuel reminded him.

"Wait a few years yet," Roman advised. "I'm sure when it's time for your *Rumschpringe* (going around with the young folks), you'll have a rig."

Lucy's thoughts were diverted from her plan to obtain the letter.

"Let's hurry and do the dishes," she encouraged Annie. "Then we can go to the box stall and see Star."

"You stay away from the barn," Father commanded. "Star may become nervous if you children traipse out there. I'll check on her several times during the night. She'll be alright."

"But can't we see her baby?" Annie asked.

"Sure, but not until I say so," Roman insisted.

Lucy mumbled something to Annie about grown-ups always being the boss. She knew she had better obey. Her parents were not abusive, but the hickory switch was no stranger to the Troyer children. It seldom needed to be used, yet Lucy had experienced its message several times.

"Oh, Lucy, just think! A baby horse," Annie exclaimed. "Right here on our very own farm. I've never seen a real one. In my other school, we had a baby animal picture book. I saw a picture of one then. Do you think we can play with it?" Annie asked.

"We only pet it," Lucy told her. "We call it a *Hutschli*, not a baby *Gaul* (horse)."

"But on our very own farm!" Annie exclaimed again.

For the first time since Pearlie Mae came to the Troyer's, Lucy felt a twinge of resentment. "It's not *your* farm," she replied, "and it won't be your *Hutschli* either."

Annie was stunned. Lucy had never spoken harshly to her before.

Noticing the hurt in Annie's eyes, Lucy relented. "Well," she said softly, "until your mother comes, we can share."

Annie didn't answer.

After the girls were in bed, Lucy remembered the letter and her plan.

"Annie," she said. "I'm making a plan about that letter. It's my secret, but I'll share it with you. Then it will be our secret." She hoped it would ease the hurt she had caused earlier.

8
What's Wrong with Annie?

Morning dawned bright and clear. The first spring crocuses were lifting dewy faces toward the sun. Everything seemed alive and new—as new as the wobbly *Hutschli* born during the night.

Annie felt like skipping, singing, and laughing all at the same time. Father had promised the children he would show them the colt.

"When?" Annie asked.

"After you have done your morning chores. The quicker your work is finished, the sooner you can see it." Then as an afterthought, Dad cautioned, "No *schusslich Arewet* (careless work) now. I expect things to be done right."

It seemed to Lucy as if old Brindle would never quit giving down her milk. Finally in exasperation, she moved on to the roan cow. To herself she was thinking, "I hope Dad doesn't notice the pail isn't quite as full."

By the time Lucy had completed her task, her father called. "Alright, *Kinner* (children), you may come quietly to see the colt. Don't run. Walk slowly to the stall. Star is rather nervous. We don't want to excite her."

It was all Lucy could do to keep from hurrying. She held her hands out to keep her brothers from getting there before she did.

"Stop it," Leon told her.

"Shh! You'd better be quiet," she warned him. "Dad doesn't want any *Yacht* (noise)."

As she came in view of the box stall, Lucy stopped. Standing beside her dad was Annie. Annie's job was to feed and water the chickens. She also filled the water pail and the warming reservoir on the side of the cookstove, which provide warm water for washing.

How did Annie get finished so soon? Lucy wondered. And why was she allowed to see the colt before anyone else? After all, she wasn't family. A surge of anger welled up within Lucy's heart.

"Oh!" exclaimed Annie. "Isn't it *schnuck* (cute)?"

"Humph," Lucy replied.

"See, it's all *schiddlich* (shaky)," Joseph observed. "Is it cold?"

"No," Roman said. "In a few hours, she'll be running and kicking up her heels."

"Oh, then it's a girl," Leon said.

"Ya," Father responded. "It's a filly.

"Es is zeit fer Friehschtick (it's time for breakfast). Let's get to the house. Now listen to me good, children. I don't want any of you to come around Star alone. You've all seen the *Hutschli*. Do you understand?"

"Yes," they replied.

"But I don't understand why Annie got to see it first," Lucy blurted out. "She isn't really one of our family."

"*Was hast du gsaat* (what did you say)?" Roman asked sternly.

"Why did Annie get to see the *Hutschli* first?" Lucy murmured, trembling.

"*Was meh* (what else) did you say?" her father demanded.

She didn't answer. Her legs seemed unable to support her.

"Come on. *Raus mit* (out with it)."

Never had her dad looked so huge to Lucy. He seemed to tower over her, waiting for her answer.

"She isn't part of our family," Lucy coughed out in a subdued tone.

"Don't ever say that again," Roman warned his daughter. "As long as she lives here, she is part of our household. It just so happened she finished her chores first. Now go on to the house. I'll settle with you later."

Lucy knew what "settle later" meant. She did not look forward to it. But she did as she was told.

Annie had already returned to the house. She felt like a whipped puppy. How she longed for her mother to come. Homesickness had plagued her before, but this was hard.

On the way to school, Lucy ran ahead of Annie. The girls generally enjoyed walking together. This morning it was different.

"We have a *Hutschli*," Lucy informed her girlhood friends. "It's so *schnuck*."

"Where's Annie?" they asked.

This did not please Lucy at all. She thought everyone would be excited at her news. Instead, they asked about Annie. It infuriated her.

"Is that all you have to say?" she asked. "Maybe you didn't hear me. I said we have a *Hutschli*, and it's so *schnuck.*"

"We heard you," Christina Beachy said. "But you and Annie always walk together."

"Is she sick?" Mabel Yoder asked.

"No, *she's* not sick, but I'm getting sick and tired of her. Everyone thinks she is so pretty. Just because she has curly hair and dimples! I wish her mom would come and get her. She still has some of her hillbilly ways. You ought to hear how she talks sometimes. And she can ask the dumbest questions."

The girls looked shocked. Never had they heard Lucy talk like this before. In fact, they thought Lucy and Annie were best of friends.

"What did Annie do?" Dena Chupp asked.

"You wouldn't understand," Lucy complained. "She gets away with everything. She isn't perfect."

"What's wrong with Annie?" the girls wondered.

Annie just shrugged her shoulders and walked along, looking glum. When they reached the schoolyard, she rushed inside, put her lunch on the shelf, and buried her head in a library book.

The other children played outside until the bell rang for school.

9
Startling News

This was Lucy's chance. Since the excitement of the new colt, she had forgotten about the letter. It was Saturday forenoon and, as usual, she was told to clean the living room. Annie was busy filling the kerosene lamps and washing the glass chimneys.

Lucy was muttering to herself, "Why does Annie always get the easy jobs? I'd rather do lamps than this old floor." She gave a quick swish with the broom.

"What's this?" She bent down and picked up a slip of paper. It was a receipt for a grain bill. Although Lucy didn't know what it was, she knew it belonged in the rolltop desk. That is where Roman kept all his business papers. The children had been told to stay out of that desk.

What was Lucy to do? Father was not in the house. Mother had her hands covered with pie dough. It would be best just to quickly open the rolltop a bit and slip the paper inside, she decided.

As quietly as possible, Lucy slid the top up a few inches. Then she saw it. There was the same gray crumpled envelope she had seen before. Here was her chance! She took the letter and quickly slipped it inside her dress pocket, under her apron.

Work seemed lighter since she had found the letter. A plan had been brewing in her mind for a while to search her dad's desk for the letter. She didn't think it would be so easy. But now she even had the excuse of wanting to return the receipt.

Lucy knew it would be risky, but she did not consider the consequences if she was found out. She planned to find a safe place to read it. Somehow she would return it to its proper place. No one need ever know. Maybe she wouldn't even tell "pet" Annie, as she now referred to her.

Singing as she swept, Lucy made short work of her cleaning. After the floor was mopped to a shine, she sought her mother.

"Mom," she said, "I'm finished, but I need to go to the *Heisli* (outhouse)." Like most Amish in their area, they didn't have an indoor bathroom.

"Well, go then, but don't sit too long," Mother said. She knew how Lucy liked to stay extra long, just to escape work, and read the old catalog kept there for toilet paper.

"Remember, you need to polish the furniture yet."

Lucy was already halfway down the walk.

"I don't see why that child wants to spend any more time than necessary in that smelly place," her Mother murmured to herself.

Clutching the envelope in her pocket, Lucy ran on.

She figured this was the most unlikely place of being discovered. Making sure the hook on the inside was securely fastened, Lucy made herself comfortable. The letter was only a half page long. The writing was smudged and dim.

Lucy began to read the poorly written letter:

To the Troyers,

My sister ast me to rite you. She giv me you adres. We cud not fine Mr. Streeter. A man at the bar say he is in prisn sum whar. Mrs. Streeter, she took the fevor sleepin' in the car and passed on. She sad fur you to kep Pearlie Mae cuz she'll git a rite smart raisin' with you folks. I hain't fittin' to take her. She's yours to kep.

—Uncle Louie

Lucy was puzzled. What did it mean? Was Annie's mother not coming back? Where did she go? The letter said she passed on. How could she solve this mystery? Lucy knew she could not ask her Mother. That would reveal her secret.

What should she do? Would Annie know what it meant? Lucy wasn't sure she wanted "pet" Annie to stay. The final decision was to return the letter to the desk. Perhaps the sooner the better.

"Annie, go see what's keeping Lucy," Mrs. Troyer requested. "I have a notion she's looking at that catalog. If she thinks she's getting out of work, she's wrong. Tell her to *mach schnell* (hurry) and get in here."

Lucy heard Annie coming and quickly replaced the envelope in her pocket.

43

"*Was wit du* (what do you want)?" she asked Annie crossly.

"Mom says *mach schnell* and get in here," Annie replied.

"Ach, I was ready to come," Lucy answered. "You didn't need to come and get me." She slammed the outhouse door, pushed Annie aside, and flounced toward the house.

"Get busy and polish the furniture," Susan said.

Only one thing about that job pleased Lucy now. This would give her a chance to put the letter back in the desk. How wrong she was!

Her father had come in early to get some checks out in the mail that day. Mr. Troyer always paid his bills on time. The mail carrier came at eleven o'clock. Roman had meant to take care of this the night before, but he fell asleep in his chair and completely forgot about it.

Lucy wished with all her heart that she had not taken the letter. Maybe he wouldn't notice that the letter was missing.

He worked awhile and started to close the desk. Then he stopped and, opening it again, he fumbled among the papers, then called to his wife.

"Susan, did you take that *Brief* (letter) out of my desk?"

"Ach no," she answered.

"Well, *ebber hot* (someone did)," he replied.

Lucy froze.

10
Smart Raisins

"Lucy, have you been *schnuppering* (snooping) in my desk?" Roman asked his daughter.

"Dad, you know we aren't allowed in your desk. But while I was cleaning in here, I saw something on the floor. I picked it up and—well, is this what you're looking for?" Lucy handed him the letter. She sincerely hoped he would believe her.

Roman snatched the letter from her hand. "Why were you hiding it in your pocket?" he asked sternly.

"Well, like you said, we're supposed to stay out of your desk," Lucy answered avoiding his eyes.

"What were you going to do with it?" her dad quizzed her.

"Give it back," she replied.

"I hope you're telling me the truth. Did you read it?"

"Ach, we aren't allowed to read your mail," Lucy replied.

"If I find out different, you are in real *Druwwel* (trouble). Now, go on and finish your work."

Lucy's hands shook so she could hardly hold the dustcloth. Annie saw how frightened she was. Why was Roman Troyer so strict with Lucy? Annie wondered. She felt sorry for Lucy.

Then she remembered that Lucy had stopped her cleaning and spent a long time in the outhouse. Perhaps she *did* read that letter. Annie decided to ask Lucy the first chance she would get.

That chance didn't come until bedtime.

"Lucy," Annie confronted her, "did you do it?"

"Did I do what?" Lucy asked innocently. She knew what Annie meant, but she was trying to stall for time while she decided how to answer.

"Did you read the letter?" Annie asked.

"You heard what I told dad. He would whip me good if I did such a thing."

"My Paw only wore me out good when he was on the jug," Annie said. "Maw told me it's 'cause he had too much to drink. He didn't know what he was doing. After he came around, he was always sorry. But, Lucy, your paw, he don't drink. Maw always said it was the moonshine whiskey what done it. I can't figure why your pappy whips you if he is sober. Don't make no sense to me."

"Well, I don't know what you mean by the jug, or moonshine whiskey," Lucy told Annie. "Dad says he loves us enough to spank us, so we learn to obey. He says we will be the better for it."

The girls still used the English language a lot. Annie was doing much better with speaking Pennsylva-

46

nia Dutch, but it was still easier for her in her native tongue.

"One thing, though, Annie. Please don't call my mom and dad 'Maw' and 'Paw' or 'Pappy.' "

"I'll try to remember," Annie promised.

Lucy couldn't sleep. Guilt weighed heavy upon her conscience. Trying to make her sin lighter, she reasoned that what she had said was partly true. *I did find a paper on the floor,* she thought. *Also, I did not tell Dad that I didn't read the letter. I only reminded him that I knew we weren't allowed to. Anyway, it wasn't really a lie.* Tossing and turning, Lucy tried to convince herself that what she had done wasn't so bad. Finally she fell into a troubled sleep.

"Wake up! Wake up!" Annie was shaking Lucy.

"What! Where am I?" Lucy asked. She sat bolt upright. Her eyes looked frightened and staring. Her hair was all disheveled. One braid was completely undone. She was sweating profusely.

"What's the matter with you?" Annie asked. "You were talking in your sleep, I guess. Over and over you said, 'Don't tell! Don't tell him I read it!' Then you begged, 'No, Dad, no. I won't do it again. I'll tear it up. Stop, Dad.' What were you dreaming?"

"Oh, leave me alone, Annie. I don't believe I said that."

"Yes, you did. I heard you. Lucy, you *did* read it, didn't you?"

Lucy could not control her emotions any longer. She began sobbing—great sobs that shook the bed. "Don't tell, Annie. Please don't."

"Then let me know what it said. Who was it from?"

"Oh, Annie, it was from your Uncle Louie. Anyway, that's how it was signed." Lucy spoke brokenly between sobs.

"Quit crying and tell me," Annie said.

"I don't remember all of it. The paper was soiled, and the spelling was hard to make out. It said your dad's in jail and your mom passed on. I don't know where, but she wants you to stay with us. Louie said we would give you raisins. I don't know why he wants you to have smart raisins," Lucy told her.

"I don't even care for raisins," Annie laughed softly. "Wish I knew what it all meant. I do miss my maw. Even though I like it here, I want her to come back."

"Don't forget now," Lucy reminded Annie again. "You won't tell."

"I promise. But I wonder if your maw—I mean mom and dad—will tell us. Seems right I should know where my mom is and why I need smart raisins. I never heard of anything like that," Annie said.

11
The Bishop's Advice

Roman and Susan felt they must speak to the bishop about keeping Annie.

"Maybe we should talk to our parents and see what they think," Susan said.

"Ya, it wouldn't be the first time they gave us good advice," Roman answered.

So they decided to make arrangements for the two of them with their parents to talk things over with the bishop, at his house.

"I'll ask him when it suits," Roman said.

The bishop was the lead minister of the church. Amish churches have several ordained ministers. The bishop regularly conferred with the other preachers, but he usually summed up the counsel.

Bishop Mose was a kind, gentle man. He shared with his flock much wisdom he had gleaned from the Bible and from faithful Christian living. Yes, it would be wise indeed to share the letter with him.

About two weeks later, the Troyers visited Bishop Mose. Both sets of parents were there also, but without knowing the reason for the meeting. No wonder Roman's and Susan's mothers were nervous. What was the meaning of this?

Seated with his guests in the living room, Bishop Mose began. Clearing his throat he said, "Well, Roman, do you want to tell us why you called us together? I hope it is not a case of family disagreement. So many people have that kind of problem. I hope it isn't so in this case."

"No, no, not at all," Roman assured him. "I can see why you thought that since I asked our parents to come along. This does concern them because Annie has been living among us. We all think highly of her. She has come a long way, but now. . . ." Roman hesitated.

"*Was hot sie geduh* (what did she do)?" the bishop asked.

"*Nix* (nothing)," Roman replied. "This letter came several weeks ago, and we want your advice. What shall we do?"

Bishop Mose took the letter. He began to read. "This is hard to make out," he said, moving closer to the kerosene lamp.

"Do you mind reading it out loud?" Roman asked.

"I'll try," Bishop Mose replied. "The spelling is not easy to decipher."

Mose began to read, fumbling at times. Eventually they got the message. Each one was shocked.

"Ach my!" exclaimed Susan's mother. "*Was tun mir* (what will we do)?"

"*Es is schrecklich* (it's scary)!" Roman's mother remarked.

"Have you told Annie yet?" the bishop asked.

"Not yet," Roman said.

"We've been putting it off because we don't know how," Susan told them.

"*Aarms Kind* (poor child)!" Hannah Schrock said.

"To complicate matters, Annie has had a bad case of homesickness lately," Roman reported.

"Yes," Susan agreed. "She keeps asking when her mother is coming back."

"Didn't you salt her or treat her for it?" Elsie Troyer asked. Grandma Elsie was one for old-time cures. Two of those included putting salt under the bedsheet and straining drinking water through a clean dishcloth. The child would then drink this water to wash away the homesickness.

Susan did not value such practices. But to appease her mother-in-law, she promised to do so.

"Has Annie been giving you any trouble?" the bishop asked.

"No," Roman said, "she hasn't."

"How does she fit in with the other children? Do they get along with each other?"

Roman waited for his wife to answer. He remembered Lucy's remark about Annie not being one of the family. How ashamed he would be to reveal this. So Susan responded to the bishop's question.

"Ya, she mostly gets along well with them. Oh, you know how it is with children. They have their scraps, but soon it's all forgotten."

"Ya, I do know how it is," Bishop Mose answered.

"If only us grown-ups were more like children, many a church split could be avoided. Our Lord teaches us that if we do not become as *die kleine Kinner* (the little children), we cannot enter the kingdom of heaven" (Matthew 18:3).

"Ya, *sel is so* (that's so)," Grandpa Troyer agreed.

"Well, back to our question at hand," the bishop reminded them, "what to do about this letter. I don't see how you can do anything at all. There is no return address. It's a sad situation. My advice to you is to give Annie the letter. It will be her only tie with her home, though a poor excuse of a home it might have been. There must be some good memories somewhere.

"Sit down with your children while Annie reads the note. Let them see her pain. I believe it will help them accept her even more. Annie has a right to know why her mother has not returned.

"How do the rest of you feel?"

They all agreed with Bishop Mose.

"Then you think Annie should stay?" Roman asked.

"Where else would she go?" Hannah Schrock asked. "I know you have your hands full with your own seven, Susan. But Annie does help with the work. Especially now, she should stay. She needs family."

Susan decided that now was not the time to tell of the conflict between Annie and their daughter Lucy. They would do all they could to work it out. Yes, with God's help, they would try. For now at least, Annie must stay.

12
All Because of a Foot-Tub

It was late when Roman and Susan returned.

"What took you so long?" Lucy asked. "Why did you go to see Bishop Mose, anyway? The baby was *gridlich* (fussy). I made Annie put her to bed, but she still fussed."

Avoiding her daughter's questions, Susan took baby Esther. "Esther is cutting teeth, and that makes her more *gridlich*," Mother explained. "You and Annie, go wash your feet and get ready for bed."

Since Amish children often run barefooted all summer, this was an evening routine. The foot-tub hung just outside the kitchen door, in the wash closet.

"Why did your mom and dad go to see the bishop?" Annie asked.

"I don't know," Lucy replied. "I guess if they want us to know, they'll tell us. You empty the water, Annie. I filled the tub, so you should carry it out. Be careful and don't slop any on the floor."

Annie didn't argue. However, she wished Lucy had not filled it so full. It was heavy. As she reached to open the screen door, the tub slipped from her hands. Dirty, soapy water ran across the floor.

"*Du dappich Maedel* (you clumsy girl)!" Lucy scolded. "Now look what you've done. You're in trouble for sure!"

At that moment Roman Troyer came in after putting his horse and buggy away for the night.

"*Was hot's do gewwe* (what happened here)?" he asked.

"Annie dropped the *Fuuss Zuwwer* (foot-tub) and spilled all the water," Lucy smugly informed her dad.

Annie stood trembling. She did not know what to expect. "I didn't mean to do it," she assured Roman.

"Of course you didn't," he agreed. His heart went out to this poor, homeless waif. Had it been proper for an Amish man to do so, he would have gathered her in his strong arms to comfort her. Instead, he spoke kindly.

"Accidents happen. Lucy, go get a bucket and the mop. Annie, ask Mom for an old *Huddel* (rag). We'll clean this up in no time."

Annie scurried to find Susan, but Lucy only stood there with her mouth gaping open. Had she heard her dad correctly? Why should she help clean up the mess? She hadn't created it. Wasn't Annie getting any punishment at all for her carelessness? Lucy couldn't believe it.

"Didn't you hear what I asked you to do?" her dad confronted her.

"Ya, Dad," she replied.

"Well then, do it. *Mach schnell* (hurry)."

Annie was already back with the *Suwwer* (tub). "I'm so sorry," she said again. Tears glistened in her eyes.

"Worse things have happened," Roman said.

Lucy appeared with a sullen look and mumbled to Annie, "Why should I have to do this? It wasn't my fault."

"What did you say?" Father asked.

"Nix," Lucy answered.

"Yes, you did. I heard you. I want to know what you said."

Lucy knew by his tone of voice that he meant business.

"I was just wondering why I have to help clean up. Annie is the one who spilled the water."

"Did you wash your feet with it?" her dad asked.

"Ya, but I didn't drop the tub," Lucy replied.

"I'll clean it up by myself," Annie offered. "Lucy is right. I did it. Really, I don't mind."

"Well, I mind," Roman said. "Lucy, I'm ashamed that you act like this. You girls help each other. That is what we do in this house. Don't poke around. It's time we all get to bed."

Susan came to see how the girls were doing. Annie had told her of the spill.

"Lucy, you let Annie mop. You take the rag and get into the corners. Sop it up real good. We don't want any left in the *Ecke* (corners)."

The girls began to work. As soon as they were alone, Lucy began to scold. "If I were the one to be so *dappich*, I would have been punished. But since it's little Pet Annie, nothing is done. 'Oh, it's just an accident,' Dad says."

"Why, Lucy," Annie reminded her. "I said it was my fault. I wanted to clean it up myself. Surely they wouldn't punish you if it would have happened to you."

"Oh, wouldn't they? Well, I know better. I've lived here longer than you. Tell me, why am I always given the harder jobs? Getting down on hands and knees to do the corners. That's harder than mopping."

"I don't know, but I would have gladly traded if you wanted to," Annie told her.

"Since you came, it doesn't seem to matter what I want," Lucy remarked.

Annie felt sad. She wanted to be Lucy's friend. It had started out so well when she came to stay with the Troyers. If only Lucy didn't feel this way. Annie wanted her to be happy. They had almost become like sisters. What had happened? Why were things changing?

Another wave of homesickness swept over Annie. If only her mother would come back. Annie knelt by the bed to pray her evening prayer. Not so Lucy. She climbed way under the covers as soon as she could.

"Aren't you saying your prayer?" Annie asked.

Lucy did not answer.

Annie, too, was silent. As she climbed into bed, she thought, *How sad—all because of a foot-tub.*

13
Annie Must Stay

Roman Troyer and his wife dreaded what they must do. It was a Sunday with no service in their district. Saturday night after meeting with Bishop Mose, they lay awake a long time.

"I believe it's best we tell Annie right after breakfast," Roman told his wife.

"Ach, so soon," Susan replied. "I thought maybe we could wait until after supper."

"You're trying to put it off. That's understandable. Since we must do it, I think it's best to get on with it. Waiting until evening would cause a sleepless night. We would all go to bed, and she would feel all alone in the dark. Annie needs us for support."

"*Du bist recht* (you are right)," Susan agreed. "But I thought we all decided to let Annie read the letter herself. She may not believe us. Are you going to tell her?"

"Only enough to soften the shock, if possible," Roman replied. "Now try to get some sleep yourself."

Neither Roman nor Susan slept well. They were not aware that upstairs someone else had a hard time sleeping. Annie tossed and turned, still hearing Lucy's stinging remarks. Why did she call her "Pet Annie"? What had happened to spoil the happy times they used to have? In fact, the Troyer boys were nicer to Annie than Lucy was. Especially Paul and Joseph. They noticed Lucy's rudeness and tried to compensate for it.

"*Kinner* (children)," Roman said after Sunday morning breakfast. "As soon as the morning work is finished, I want everyone in the living room. So girls, get the dishes cleared away. Boys, put the horses in the east pasture. Keep Star and her colt in the feedlot."

"Are we getting company today?" Leon asked.

"No, not today," Susan said. "Just get your things done up and come inside."

"Why do you suppose we are all supposed to come to the living room?" Annie asked Lucy.

"I don't know, but the sooner you dry these dishes, the sooner we'll know."

Lucy always washed and made Annie dry. Both of them preferred washing. But rather than argue, Annie let Lucy have her way.

Eventually all the tasks were accomplished and everyone had gathered in the living room.

"Sit down, children, and be quiet," Roman instructed. He paused and cleared his throat. When he did this, they knew he had something important to say.

"Mom and I have something to tell you children. It is sad news, and it concerns Annie. We wish we would not need to do this. But Annie has a right to know."

Lucy had a pretty good idea what was coming, but she kept quiet. She had seen the old envelope her dad held in his hand.

"Annie, this letter is from your uncle. Why don't you read it for us?"

"For me?" Annie said, her eyes wide with surprise.

"Ya, for you. Read it so all of us can hear," Roman said.

Slowly Annie began. She also had difficulty with the spelling. When at last she finished, she began asking questions.

"What is prison? Where is it?"

"Prison is a place they keep people locked up who need help," Roman answered. "I don't know where it is. There are many prisons."

"Where did my maw go? Uncle Louie said she passed on. She wouldn't go on without me. Why does she want you to give me smart raisins? I don't like raisins. I hardly know my uncle. Maw—I mean my mom—wouldn't give me to you for keeps. Someone made this up. Lucy made it all up. She doesn't like me anymore," Annie sobbed.

"Come here," Susan said. Annie ran to the rocker where Susan sat holding little Esther. Susan, too, was crying.

"Oh, Annie. I'm so sorry. The letter is true. Your Mother died from a fever. That's what your uncle meant when he said she passed on. Before your mother died, she asked that we keep you and raise you right."

"I don't believe it!" Annie cried. "Why wouldn't

they bring her back so I could see her?"

"We don't know, Annie," Roman told her. "Without a return address, we have no way of reaching Louie. Do you have any other relatives?"

"My maw—mom, I mean Mother, showed me a picture once of a fancy lady. She told me it was her sister Myrtle. I don't know where she lived. Because we were poor, Myrtle never came to see us. Mom said she wanted 'no truck' with our kind. Said she wasn't Christian, so I guess she's a heathen. Anyway, I want my Mother!" Annie burst into a fresh spell of crying.

"Have you been happy here, Annie?" Susan asked.

"Most of the time," Annie replied. "You treat me good. I'll stay here and wait for my mom. Maybe Louie made a mistake. He don't write so good. But what if Lucy doesn't want me to stay?" Annie asked.

"Now, why wouldn't she want you?" Susan said.

Before Annie could answer, Lucy spoke up. "Of course I want you to stay. We all do, don't we?" she asked her brothers and sisters.

"Oh, yes," they chorused. "Annie must stay."

They all agreed. And it was so. Annie would stay.

14

I Aim to Know

Mrs. Troyer did not have the heart to send Annie to school on Monday morning.

"Please, I don't want to go," Annie begged. *"Miss ich* (do I have to)?"

"I'll talk to Dad about it," Susan said.

"Oh, Roman, I just can't make her go," she told her husband later.

"Well, I don't know," he replied. "She'll have to face it sometime. We feel sorry for her, but she can't use this to get her own way."

"Generally when there is a death among our people, they're given three days to adjust and start to grieve," Susan reminded him.

"Ya, *sel is waahr* (that is true). Let her stay then."

Annie was grateful. All day she followed Susan around the house and yard. Monday is wash day for Amish women. Mechanically, Annie helped with the laundry. She kept the clothes from tangling up in the wringer, handed Susan the clean clothes and pins, and watched baby Esther.

Question after question poured forth as she followed Susan.

"Why didn't Uncle Louie come get me? Don't you think my mom would have told him to come? Do you think she had to sleep in our rickety old car? Was the fever she had real bad? Louie would have taken her to the doctor. He couldn't leave her in that old car to die, could he?

"If my mom did die, where is she now? When Granny Wolfe from our church died, they buried her in the churchyard. Where do you think my mom's burying place is? I want to go and see it. I have to, so I'll know."

To the flood of Annie's questions, there was only one answer. That answer was three hopeless words: "I don't know."

"Well," Annie stated, "I don't know either, but I'm bound to find out."

"You have a right to know," Susan said. "I wish your uncle would have come and told us more. Since he didn't, we can only hope and pray. It is almost time to start lunch. You must be hungry. You hardly ate anything since yesterday."

"I'm not hungry. I don't want to eat," Annie said.

"You must eat. The way it is now, you are so thin. We must keep your strength up. Bring Esther along to the kitchen. We'll make *Schnitz un Gnepp*."

This is a dish similar to chicken and dumplings. Ham is used instead of chicken. The *Schnitz* are dried apple slices, and the *Gnepp* are dumplings. They consist of flour, baking powder, salt, eggs, butter, and milk. Although one of Annie's favorite foods, it failed to delight her.

Annie was just as quiet at the table as she had been talkative before. Again she ate little. Brushing aside her tears, she found it hard to swallow.

"Is that all you're eating?" Paul asked.

Annie didn't answer.

"Tell you what," Paul said. "Dad wants me to go to Brumly for roofing nails. If it's alright with Mom and Dad, you can come along."

Annie had never ridden in an open buggy. This was the first sign of interest she had shown.

"*Maeg ich* (may I)?" Annie asked.

"Are you sure, Paul?" Roman asked.

"Of course. It would be company for me. What do you say, Mom?"

Roman looked at Susan. She smiled and nodded her consent.

"It's settled then," Roman told Annie. "You may go."

"*Denki* (thanks)," Annie responded. "I'll quickly help with the dishes," she told Paul. "Wait for me."

"Don't worry. You'll probably be ready before I am. First I must bring Babe in from the pasture. She isn't always willing to come."

"Why don't you take Dep?" Roman suggested. "She's in the barn already."

"Dad, I'd as soon walk as take Dep. She is so slow. She only has one gait, and that is creeper gear."

"*Es is net so schlimm* (it isn't that bad)," Susan told Paul. "I drive her all the time. She gets me there and back in one piece."

Annie wished they would take Babe. She had seen her run. It must be fun to ride behind such a fast horse.

"Babe needs to be driven more," Paul reminded his dad.

"Well, if you want the bother of catching her, it's alright."

Annie felt excited and quite grown up. She was glad Paul wanted her along for company. On the way, they had lots of time to chat.

"Paul, do you think it's true?" Annie asked.

"Do I think what's true?" he asked her.

"You know. About my mom."

"All I know is what the letter said."

"Last night I remembered that I have a birthday next week. Now my mother isn't even here when I'm ten. I wish she could come. She always baked a cake for me."

"My, my. You will be ten! Soon you'll be a young lady. I'll see what I can do about your birthday. It's a bit early, but why not celebrate today? After I finish at the hardware, we will do something special—just for you," Paul promised.

"What is it? Tell me! Tell me!" begged Annie.

"It's a warm day. Babe needs a little rest before we start home. What say we stop at Ralph's Drugstore for an ice-cream cone?"

"I say that would be fine," Annie agreed.

"Let's do it then," Paul grinned.

Not many eighteen-year-old boys would have been so thoughtful. Roman and Susan had taught their children love and compassion. It was bearing fruit.

On the way home, Annie felt better. She had made her cone last as long as she could, savoring each lick and each bite.

"Paul," she said, "no one has any answers for me. There has to be someone somewhere who knows what happened. I have to know if it's true that Mom is gone. As soon as I can, I aim to know. I don't know how, but I'll find out."

Paul grinned and nodded but didn't say anything. Babe was really hitting her stride on the homeward track, and he was busy trying to keep her under control.

15
The Surprise

Lucy felt kinder toward Annie. That is, until she heard about the day's events.

"Oh, Lucy," Annie told her. "Guess what? I went to town with Paul today. He took the open buggy, and we drove Babe. She runs so fast. It felt as if we were flying."

An open buggy is a topless carriage. The boys use it once they are of *rumschpringing* age (sixteen). It only seats two people.

"I told Paul my birthday is next week. He said since Mom won't be here for me, we would celebrate early. Guess what he did?" Annie said.

"*Ich wees net* (I don't know)," Lucy replied.

"He bought me an ice-cream cone. We sat at a counter in Ralph's Drugstore to eat them. Only I tried to make mine last as long as I could. So I ate the last of it on our way home. It was strawberry. I've never had strawberry, have you?"

"No, and Paul never bought me a cone either," she answered curtly.

Annie sensed resentment in Lucy's voice. "Maybe for your next birthday he will buy one for you," Annie said hopefully. She sincerely wanted Lucy to enjoy a day with Paul as she had.

At the supper table, talk turned to the events of the day.

"While you were gone, Paul, Dawdy Schrocks stopped by. Grandma has more *Buckelweh* (backache) again," Susan told her son. "They had been to the chiropractor. Grandpa said to tell you and Annie that they are sorry you were gone."

"Oh yes," Joseph told Annie, "Teacher said she missed you, too. She hopes you come back soon."

"Did you tell her why I don't want to come?" Annie asked.

"Well, yes," Joseph said. "She asked, and I couldn't lie."

"You did right, son," Roman assured him. "There's no reason to hide it. Annie did no wrong. You may tell Miss Zook that Annie will be in school on Wednesday."

"Grandma told me Elva Garver is looking for a *Kindsmaad* (baby-sitter)," Susan said. "She mostly needs one during chore time. They're milking twelve cows by hand. Her husband says he can't afford to pay what farmhands ask for. Eight dollars a week! *Denk mol* (think once)! That is besides room and board!"

"We sure are *glicklich* (lucky) we have our own help. Right, boys?" Roman stated.

"Sure, Dad," they agreed.

"And we get the best cooking around." Paul laughed, taking another helping of food.

"I can see why Elva needs help," Susan continued. "At chore time, she has to drag the little ones along to the barn. In the morning, she told me, she makes so many trips to the house checking to see if they're awake.

"It seemed funny to hear Grandma tell it. She said Elva joked that the grass between the house and barn needed no mowing. She said she milks one cow, then tells the next one to wait. 'I'll be right back,' she tells it."

"Do the cows understand?" Bertha asked.

"Of course not!" Leon laughed.

"Ach, that Elva Garver likes to kid around," Roman said. "But it is good to talk to the cows. They're easier to work with that way."

"At least she has a sense of humor," Paul remarked.

"Ya, I suppose some people would let it get them down," Roman said.

After most of the family was in bed, Paul approached his mom. "Today Annie told me she has a birthday next week. I believe it's the fourth of the month. She said her mom used to bake a cake for her. Annie is really feeling it that her mom can't be here for her birthday. I was wondering—would it be too much trouble to have a cake? Something special like ice cream, maybe? What do you say?"

"I say it's kind of you, Paul, to want to do such a nice thing," Susan replied. "Let me ask Dad before we make too many plans."

Roman agreed that this was a good idea. "This may

be just what Annie needs," he told his wife. "It would help her see that we care. There are still several blocks of ice left in the cave. Yes, I guess we can do it."

"The only way we can surprise her is to keep it among the three of us," Paul proposed.

"Well, I'll bake the cake after the family is in bed," Susan decided.

"I'll freeze the ice cream before the children get home from school," Paul offered. "You just get the mix ready, and I'll do the rest. It won't matter if I quit work early one time—especially for such a good reason."

"You can freeze it out in the feedway," Roman told Paul. "Once it's good and solid, cover it with the gunny sack and the leftover ice. To be sure it doesn't melt, pile straw around and on top of it."

"Let's invite both Dawdys (sets of grandparents)," Susan suggested.

"*Du was du wit* (do what you like)," Roman told his wife.

The next week everything worked out as planned. Wednesday evening found a happy group gathered around the table.

"Why did Dawdys come on a weekday?" Lucy asked her mother. "They just came on our in-between *Gmee* (church) Sunday."

"Well, this is a special time," Susan answered.

"What do you mean, special?" Lucy said.

"Wait and see," her mother responded. With that remark she looked at Paul and said, "*Es is Zeit* (it's time)."

Going to the pantry, she returned, carrying a cake with ten lit candles. Such a sight her children had never seen! They gazed in awe and surprise. Then Paul appeared with the ice-cream canister and placed it in the sink.

"Especially for you, Annie!" he said.

"Surprise! Surprise!" the grown-ups said. "Happy birthday, Annie."

16
The Wish

"Oh!" Annie exclaimed, clapping her hands. "You made this special for me?"

Baby Esther was clapping her hands, too.

"We want you to know we care," Susan told the happy girl. "You've had some sad days lately. It's time you have better ones."

"Ya," agreed Grandma Schrock. "I brought you a little something." She handed Annie a small package.

"Oh, *was is es* (what is it)?" Annie asked, reaching for the gift.

"Open it," Dawdy Schrock said.

Annie couldn't unwrap it fast enough. "Look!" she exclaimed. "It's a *Schnuppduch* (handkerchief) with pink flowers. Pink is my favorite color. *Denki Mammi* (thanks, Grandma)!" she told Grandma Schrock.

Amish girls do not wear pink, but it is permitted on hankies, dresser scarves, and quilts or pillow edging.

"Here is a small present from us, too." Grandma

Troyer said as she held it out for Annie.

"*Denki, Mammi!*" Annie exclaimed again. Excitedly she broke the string and opened a box of squares for a sampler. "It will be my very first sampler. Look, Lucy. Look at the different colors. Won't it be pretty?"

Lucy didn't comment.

A sampler is like a quilted wall hanging. A girl's first sampler was twelve inches square and made of small pieced blocks of cloth. Every young girl needed to work on a sampler. Later it would benefit her in the art of quilt making.

"I've made you this chore apron," Susan said. "But I didn't get it wrapped."

"I don't care," Annie beamed. "I would have thrown the paper away anyhow. Oh, I like this big pocket. Look, the apron fits fine." She slipped it over her dress.

"It's dark blue and won't show the dirt as much," Susan told her.

"My new handkerchief fits in the pocket, too. But I'm putting that away for Sunday use only," Annie decided, smoothing out its corners.

"It's time for the eats," Roman informed his wife.

"Leave it to the men to remind us of that," laughed Susan. "Lucy, you get the bowls set out for ice cream. Bertha, why don't you count out enough *Leffele* (spoons). I'll cut the cake."

Susan started to remove a candle when Annie called out, "Wait! Wait! I'm supposed to blow out the candles and make a wish."

Roman looked at her rather sternly. Never had he heard of such a thing.

"Oh, my mom always told me to make a wish," Annie said.

"Well, we have no such practice," Roman told her. He looked at the grandparents. "What do you think?" he asked.

Grandpa Troyer stroked his long, white beard. He sat as if in deep thought. Looking at Annie's half-doubtful expression, his heart melted. "She hasn't been with us very long. We must give her *Zeit* (time) to learn our ways."

"*Du bist recht* (you're right)," Dawdy Schrock agreed.

"Well then, *yuscht* (just) this once," Roman told Annie. "*Yuscht* so her ways don't rub off on our children," he added.

Annie waited, thinking of her wish. The others watched her.

"Go on, Annie, blow out your candles," Paul encouraged her.

The cake and ice cream were delicious. Annie felt almost happy again.

After everyone had their fill, the grown-ups visited. It was a pleasant evening, so the children played outside. *Blindemeisel* (blindman's buff) was one of their favorite games.

As shadows deepened, the grandparents left for home. Now the fireflies were lighting up the yard as they flitted about.

"Let's get some jars and catch lightning bugs," Leon suggested.

How they laughed as they jumped and grabbed at these elusive sprites. Yet all play must come to an end, and so did theirs. Darkness reached out toward them from the shade trees.

"Come now, children," Susan called from the porch. "Time to wash those dirty feet and get to bed. Tomorrow is a school day, you know."

"It won't be long until colder weather is here," Joseph said. "We won't need to wash our feet then, for we will be wearing shoes."

"You mean you don't wash your feet when you wear shoes?" Annie asked. "Not ever?"

"You know better. Of course we do, only not so often," Joseph laughed.

They took turns carrying and emptying water until the last foot was washed. This time Annie was extra careful. She had not forgotten another day and the foot-tub episode.

After the girls were in bed awhile, Annie nudged Lucy. "Are you awake, Lucy?" she asked.

"What do you want?" Lucy replied.

"I can't sleep," Annie told her. "Wasn't it a fun day?"

"Maybe for you," Lucy snapped.

"Why, Lucy, what do you mean? I thought it was a lot of fun."

"Ya, sure you would," Lucy retorted. "Who got all the presents? We never have cake and ice cream when any of us children have birthdays. And then a cake with candles yet. It's not Amish.

"And whoever heard of making a wish on a cake? But then, you're a pet. What did you wish for, Pet Annie? Tell me!"

Annie was smitten. With downcast face, she

murmured, "I can't tell you my wish or it won't come true."

"Well, it won't happen anyway, so there!" Lucy predicted.

Annie covered her face, and the hot tears fell unrestrained. Her wish had to come true. It just had to! She would tell it to no one. Not ever!

17
Lucy Spoils the Joy

Annie heard her singing. Susan liked to sing. She sang as she worked. She sang while rocking the baby, while working in the garden, and even doing laundry. It seemed unusual to hear her sing so early in the morning.

Annie was just now waking from a night of restless sleep. Mrs. Troyer was singing a German hymn. Annie could not understand the words, but the tune sounded beautiful.

How Annie wished she were as happy as Susan sounded. For awhile last night she was, but the memory of Lucy's comments had squelched her joy. Now she heard Mr. Troyer call the family to their morning chores.

"Come on, everybody. Up and at 'em," he said, tapping the stovepipe with the poker. "Chore time. I want no stragglers this morning!"

Annie jumped out of bed and began dressing. She

wanted to challenge Lucy to a race downstairs, as they often did. Glancing at Lucy's scowling face, Annie decided to go ahead.

She snatched her new chore apron from a chair and ran downstairs. After she splashed cold water on her face, she felt more awake.

"Did you sleep good?" Susan asked.

"No, I didn't," Annie truthfully replied.

"You were probably too excited from last night's surprise. Well, maybe you will sleep better tonight once you settle down. You were surprised, weren't you?"

"Oh, yes. And it was a larp—I mean, a very nice party," Annie assured Susan.

"Where is Lucy? She should be down here by *des Zeit* (this time). Was she still in bed?"

"I think she was ready to get up," Annie answered uneasily. "May I go now?" She took the water pail and started for the outdoor pump.

"Ach, of course. I'll call Lucy again. Why can't she get to her chores like you do?"

Annie wished Mrs. Troyer had not made that remark. She did not want Lucy to hear it. Although Annie was only ten, she sensed Lucy was beginning to resent her.

As the family sat at breakfast, activities of the day were discussed.

"Paul, you and I will work on repairing the round corncrib today," Roman informed his oldest son. "Better get it done before corn husking starts.

"Joseph, we need to mow the pasture one more time. Can't let those thistles get ahead of us.

"Leon, as soon as you get home from school, start cleaning the calf pens."

"Sounds like all the work around here is for us boys," Joseph teased.

"Ya," Leon joined in, "what shall the girls do?"

"Never you mind," their mother said. "I'll have work waiting for them. Just see to it that you do yours."

"Work waiting, you say," laughed Joseph. "I'll bet it will be doing just that. Waiting and waiting and waiting. You know what they say: 'Women's work is never done.' "

How the boys laughed!

"They'll get it done alright," Susan replied. "Annie couldn't get to her chores quick enough this morning. In fact, she was feeding the chickens by the time Lucy came downstairs!"

"Oh, I can't wait to get to school and tell your friends about your surprise last night," remarked Leon. "It was a nice time."

Annie wished they would talk about something else. She felt like crying again.

Lucy ran ahead of Annie on their way to school. It didn't matter. Annie preferred walking alone until the Beachy and Chupp girls joined her. They both lived between the Troyers and Button Shoe School.

At recess Lucy spent much of her time telling the girls what a "pet" Annie was.

"All my life I've lived with my family. I work hard, too. Did they ever have a surprise for my birthday? No, not once! Now here Annie comes along, and boy, look what she gets!

"Mom made a cake that looked so *englisch* (non-

Amish), with candles on it yet. Paul made a freezer of ice cream.

"Dawdys came and brought presents. She got a handkerchief with pink flowers, a box of material to make a sampler, and a new chore apron."

"You must have had a good time, though," Mabel Yoder remarked.

"Sounds like fun to me," agreed Ellen Maust.

"Fun for Annie, but not for me," Lucy complained. "I don't think it's fair."

Annie was sitting alone on the schoolhouse steps. By the looks Lucy directed her way, she knew she was being talked about. Closing her lunch pail, she went inside. Miss Zook looked up from the papers she was grading.

"Don't you want to play outside?" she asked Annie.

"No," Annie replied sadly.

Miss Zook had been informed by a note from Mrs. Troyer concerning Annie's absence. Her heart ached for this girl.

Every day after noon recess, Miss Zook read from a children's Bible storybook.

"Would you like to choose today's story?" she asked Annie.

Annie took the book. Leafing through it, she selected the story of the Prodigal Son, from Luke 15. Miss Zook read the story and called attention to the sin of the older brother. Jealousy was his problem. God spoke to the youngsters through the story.

Even though Lucy felt a twinge of guilt, she did not repent. In front of the family, her mother had praised

Annie for getting to her chores first that morning.

We'll see who gets there first tonight, she thought.

As was Annie's custom, she stopped to use the outhouse before the walk home. Lucy saw her chance and latched the door from the outside. Then she ran home as fast as she could.

18
A Mean Trick

Annie pushed and pushed on that door but it didn't even budge. *Who would play such a trick?* she wondered. Right away she thought of Lucy. She had not seen her do it, so she must not jump to conclusions.

What should Annie do? She began calling out.

"Help! Let me out," she yelled as she pounded on the door with her fists. But who would hear her?

By now the scholars had left the schoolyard. Miss Zook had locked up early and left, urging her pupils to hurry. She saw storm clouds building up in the west.

"*Kinner* (children)," she said, "*mach schnell* (hurry) and try to get home before it rains."

No one noticed that Annie was missing. Goodbyes were called out as each family's children turned in their own lane. Lightning flashed and thunder rumbled in the distance. The wind picked up in strength, with wild gusts driving dust and light trash along.

Miss Zook was glad her house was farthest from the school. She felt relieved when she could see that her charges had made it safely home.

"See you tomorrow," she called to the Yoder children. The wind caught her words and carried them away. Wrapping her shawl closely around her, she struggled the rest of the way.

Gusts of wind tugged at her bonnet. How suddenly the storm had come! Miss Zook turned into her lane and walked with her back to the wind, struggling to keep on her feet.

"Whee!" she exclaimed as she entered the kitchen. "Mom, am I ever glad to get out of that wind! Sure makes for a storm."

"Did all the *Schulkinner* (schoolchildren) make it home?" her mother asked.

"All those living out our way did. I'm sure the Mast and Byler children did, too. The Troyer children don't have far. I told them to hurry. They took off running, so I feel they are safely at home by now."

Little did Miss Zook realize that one terrified child was left behind.

Now the storm broke in all its fury. Lightning flashed hotly, and crashes of thunder split the air. Rain pelted the tin roof above Annie's head. The huge oak tree outside the door seemed to groan in the wind.

Soon hail mixed with rain added to the dreadful noises. Annie huddled in a corner on the floor. Covering her ears with her trembling hands, she cried in terror.

"Oh, Maw, why don't you come for me? As soon as I can, I'll come and find you."

Then Annie remembered a Bible verse her mother had taught her. "Whenever I'm afraid," she had told Pearlie Mae, "I will trust in the Lord."

"Yes," Annie said, "I will say it out loud. Whenever I am afraid, I will trust in you, Lord. Whenever I am afraid . . ."

But Annie was afraid. "Please, someone come and help me out of here," she sobbed.

At the Troyer home, the children rushed inside and Mom said, "*Ich bin froh das der da heim sint* (I'm glad you're home)!" The screen door slammed shut with a bang. A plastic bucket tumbled across the gravel driveway. Small limbs blew helter-skelter across the yard.

"Look, Mom," Leon exclaimed, "Duke's house fell over!" Duke was the family dog.

"Ya, such a storm it is," Susan remarked.

Roman and the older boys came in just as the rain began to fall. "We fastened everything down at the barn," Roman said. "I think the animals will be safe. The main thing is that all the children are home. Miss Zook was smart to dismiss early. I hope this isn't a twister. We will just wait it out. Chores can wait this evening."

"All the children," Mr. Troyer had said. For the first time something dawned in Susan's mind.

"Where's Annie?" she asked, suddenly alarmed. "I haven't seen Annie since school. Didn't she come with you, Lucy?"

"Miss Zook told us to run, so I ran as fast as I could," Lucy answered with pretended innocence, but without looking her mom in the face.

"Did any of you see her?" Roman asked.

"No, Dad, we didn't," they answered.

"The wind was blowing so hard, it was all we could do to walk," Leon reported. "We couldn't even hear each other talk. With all the dust flying around, we could hardly stand to have our eyes open enough to find our way."

"Oh, Roman, where do you suppose she is?" Susan wondered.

"I don't know, but I must go look for her," he replied.

"I'll go with you, Dad," Paul offered.

"We can't take the top-buggy in this wind," Roman stated. "It would tip over. Let's hitch Dep to the open buggy. She's not as skittish as Babe."

"You'll get all wet in the open buggy," Susan lamented.

"Can't be helped," her husband responded as he pulled on his coat.

Paul dashed out to hitch up Dep to his open buggy. It was a hard drive back to the school. Dep strained against the gale. There was no use trying to talk as they struggled on.

When they neared the little outhouse, they heard a scream. Annie had heard the noise of the buggy wheels and Dep's whinny.

"Help!" she called above the rattle of the storm. "Get me out! Please let me out!"

Roman reined in his horse. Paul jumped from the buggy and ran to release the captive girl. Sobbing and trembling, she fell into his strong arms.

Roman tied Dep to a rail, and the three found shelter in the small outside entranceway of the schoolhouse till the storm let up.

"Who did this to you?" Paul asked.

"I don't know," Annie said.

"Well, someone latched that door on the outside, and I aim to find out who did it. It was a mean trick. We'll get to the bottom of this."

"The main thing is, we found you," Roman declared. "As soon as the rain lets up, we'll get you home. Mom is worried. Thank God you're safe now."

"What a mean trick!" Paul remarked again.

19
Annie's Rescue

When the storm subsided, Lucy hurried to her chores. To throw off any suspicion directed against herself, she started on Annie's work also.

Amish farms provided many tasks. Each young child was given a work assignment, which helped to create a bond of belonging in the family. So Lucy knew exactly what Annie's chores were.

As the buggy came down the drive, Mrs. Troyer breathed a sigh of relief. "Ach my!" she exclaimed as she opened the screen door to let Annie inside quickly. "You're soaked. Go change into *drucken gleeder* (dry clothes)."

Annie started crying. She was still frightened as she trudged up the stairs.

"Come down as soon as you have changed," Susan called after her, "and I'll give you a cup of good, hot peppermint tea. That will help warm you up." She moved the teakettle to the hottest part of the stove.

Roman and Paul came sloshing in as soon as Dep was bedded down.

"*Was hot's gewwe* (what happened)?" Susan asked her husband. "Where did you find Annie?"

"Someone had shut her up in the outhouse," Paul answered. "The outside latch was hooked."

"Ach no!" Susan exclaimed. "Who would do such a thing? She must have been terribly afraid."

"Yes, she was," Roman replied.

"*Aarm Kind* (poor child)! Alone through all that storm! As if she hasn't been through enough," Susan lamented.

"Well, I am going to find out who did it, one way or another," Paul vowed. He didn't have long to wait.

"You two had better get into dry clothes or you'll both get sick," Susan told them. "I've got hot tea ready."

Still wiping tears and visibly shaken, Annie sat down to drink her tea. Her hands trembled so much that she had difficulty holding the cup. The men soon joined her.

"How about some half-moon pie to go with our tea," Paul suggested.

"Ya," Roman agreed. "Maybe Annie would want some, too."

However, Annie didn't want pie. She only drank the tea to help warm up.

Just then Lucy came bursting through the door.

"As soon as we finish our tea, Paul, we'd better hustle to our chores. We're running a little late," Dad said.

Now is my chance to shine, Lucy thought. *Maybe*

they'll see Annie is not the only important one.

"I've already finished my chores, all except milking. Then, because I felt sorry for Annie being locked up in that old outhouse, I did some of hers. I even—"

She was interrupted by her dad as he arose from his chair. Towering over Lucy, he demanded in an even but firm tone, "What did you say?"

"I did some of Annie's chores because she was locked up in the outhouse," Lucy answered.

"You just now came in and did not hear us talking. Is that right?" her father asked.

"Ya, Dad, I was out doing chores. I went as soon as the storm let up a little," she answered.

"This is the first you came into the house since Paul, Annie, and I got back?" her father questioned further.

"Why, yes, Dad. I told you. Didn't I do good to do part of Annie's work?"

"How did you know Annie was penned up in the outhouse?" Roman asked.

Everything was completely silent as they waited for Lucy's explanation. She felt hot and then cold as she realized that she had betrayed herself.

"*Ich bin am waarde* (I'm waiting)," her dad said.

"I just knew that Annie always goes to the *Heisli* (outhouse) before starting home," Lucy replied feebly.

"But how did you know the door was hooked from the outside?" he demanded.

Lucy didn't know what to say. She began to squirm and cry.

"You did it, didn't you?" her dad asked, watching her closely.

Guilt was written all over her face. She couldn't look up.

"I am asking you once more. Did you hook that door, knowing Annie was in there?"

There was no way out. It was too evident. Crying harder because she had been caught, Lucy replied with a nod of her head.

"Why did you do such a thing?" Roman asked his daughter.

"You . . . you . . . ," sobbed Lucy. "Everyone likes Annie best. You made a surprise for her birthday. Paul took her along to town in his open buggy. I never had a birthday cake or went to town with Paul. Mom thinks Annie works better than me. Why does she have to live here?"

"Lucy, I'm ashamed of your attitude," Roman reprimanded her. "You are our child, and we think as much of you as any of the others, including Annie. It sounds to me as if you are giving in to jealousy. That is a terrible sin.

"I can hardly believe you would do such a cruel thing as you did to Annie. After supper we will deal with this matter. Annie needs special attention at this time. She has just lost her mother. I hope we can get you to understand."

Annie was beginning to feel like a troublemaker. If she hadn't come to live with the Troyer's, Lucy would not be in for punishment. *I must leave*, she thought.

She remembered her mother and her Leaning Tree. Yes, that's where she would go. She'd go there tomorrow.

20

The Leaning Tree

Lucy was severely punished. Roman Troyer did not enjoy using the strap. But he believed Proverbs (22:15; 23:13-14) that the rod of correction would drive out foolishness.

After supper Dad called Lucy to the porch and talked about these verses with her.

"Lucy, the Bible says that foolishness is bound up in the heart of a child, but correction will deliver the child. These are strong instructions. I am not going to beat you, but I will strap you enough to set your feet on the right path."

Annie cringed at each outcry Lucy made. She covered her ears to shut out the sound of the strap. It brought back memories of the beatings her mother suffered from a drunken husband.

Flinging herself into Susan's arms, she begged, "Stop! Oh, make him stop! I'll go away. Then Lucy won't get whipped."

"Hush," Susan said, stroking Annie's head. "He isn't strapping her anymore. Look, Lucy is sitting beside him on the swing."

"What is Dad telling her?" Annie asked.

"I can't hear him, but I suppose he is explaining why he whipped her."

"And why is that? Couldn't he have punished her some other way?"

"Yes, he could have," Susan replied. "It probably would not have made such a lasting impression as this will. Some children need more correction than others. I'm afraid Lucy is such a child." Mom reached up and brushed a tear away.

"I wish Lucy would like me again. When I first came, we had so much fun. What did I do?"

"*Nix* (nothing), Annie," Susan reassured her. "You did not do a thing to bring this change. Lucy has a bad case of jealousy."

"Maybe I should live someplace else."

"No! You're family, and you belong right here."

However, Annie kept thinking things over. She had been back to her family's tenant house earlier, but it was locked. It could hardly be called a house. Some called it Streeter's Shack. It was more like a cabin, but to Annie it had been home.

As she focused her mind on that home, a few good memories lingered. It was hardly more than a mile from the Troyer farm. Situated in Button Shoe Hollow, the top of the chimney was barely visible from the Troyer farm. A large old cottonwood tree sheltered it and provided shade. Annie had played under its branches many times.

Here her mother came when life's burdens became too heavy to bear. She would lean wearily against its strong trunk. Looking to the hills beyond the hollow, she found strength.

Those hills were known as Button Shoe Ridge, but to Annie and her mother, they were God's Hills. They had given the tree a name, the Leaning Tree.

Once Annie had questioned her mother about it.

"Maw," she had asked, "why do you call the cottonwood the Leaning Tree?"

"Pearlie Mae," Mrs. Streeter told her, "when I am sad and the cares of life are too much for me, I come here for help. If I have quarreled with your paw, I find forgiveness here."

"But how, Maw?" Pearlie Mae asked.

"At meetin', Preacher Joel says to do as the Good Book says. 'I will lift up my eyes to the hills; from which my help comes. My help comes from the Lord, who made heaven and earth.' That's found in Psalm 121. The preacher says to read it and obey. So that's what I try to do.

"I lean on this tree and look to God's Hills, waiting for strength from the Lord. He gives it, child. Yes, God does help us. Always remember that."

Annie remembered now. She needed the Leaning Tree. Quietly she crept out of bed that night. Picking up her clothes and shoes, she made her way carefully downstairs. Softly she stole outside to the washhouse.

There by the light of a waning moon, she dressed. Now she would wait until daybreak. Annie was sure this was best. Her plans were to find some way to get into the empty cabin, maybe through a window. She was sure she could do it.

Annie knew her mother had canned many jars of wild berries and dried herbs before she left. Those things would be food enough for her, she figured. Anyway, Annie felt certain that her mother would return any day now.

At the first streak of light, Annie hurried across the buggy yard. She kept to the ditch at the roadside. Her shoes got wet from the dew as she ran. At the first sight of the cabin, Annie's heart began to beat rapidly. The door was standing wide open.

"Maw," she called, racing wildly down the slope into the hollow. "Maw! Maw, you came home! Where are you?"

Everything was silent. Annie looked everywhere. She called and called, but in vain. Then she noticed that all the windows had been shattered. The few remaining pieces of furniture were thrown on the floor and smashed. Her mother's old rocker lay in pieces. Someone had broken into the cabin and taken what they wanted.

Disappointed and blinded by tears, Annie ran to the cottonwood. She leaned against its huge trunk and looked toward the hills.

The sun was just coming up over the ridge. Its shades of gold and pink were beautiful, but Annie found no comfort in them. She clung to the tree, crying until she was spent.

After searching frantically, that is exactly where Paul and Joseph found her later that morning.

"Annie, what are you doing here?" Paul asked. "We were so worried."

"I thought maybe Maw would come back if I would be here," Annie told them. "Someone broke into our house.

"I thought if I went away, Lucy wouldn't get punished any more. The Leaning Tree was supposed to help, but it doesn't."

Paul didn't know what she meant. "Let's go home," he said. "You must be hungry. Mom saved some breakfast for you."

21

The Locket

Annie felt her return to the cabin had not been in vain. Hidden deep within her pocket underneath her apron, she carried a treasure.

Something had caught her eye as she left the house and ran to the old cottonwood. Lying on the mantel above the fireplace, it glistened in the morning sun. It was the locket containing her mother's picture.

Annie had seen it many times before. To her, it was so beautiful with its imitation gold chain. Why would her mother leave it behind? She was thankful that it had not been taken. Quickly she had slipped it into her pocket. Never would she part with it!

Annie was well aware that the Amish have a rule against photographs. They say it's a violation of God's commandment not to make any graven image or likeness. Well, Amish or not, Annie was determined to keep the locket with its picture.

If she was to keep it, she knew she would have to

hide it. But—maybe if she showed it to Lucy, Lucy would like her better. Annie liked being Amish, and she did want to be Lucy's friend again.

One day when Lucy was being especially difficult, Annie made her decision.

"Lucy, I have something to show you if you'll be my friend again, . . . and if you promise you won't tell. It'll be our very own secret."

"What is it?" Lucy asked. The girls were preparing for bed, but neither one was sleepy.

"Promise you won't tell and that we will be friends again?"

"Is it something good?" Lucy wondered, not ready to commit herself.

"It's real good," Annie assured her.

"Alright, I promise," Lucy answered.

Annie went to the dresser and opened a drawer, reaching deep into the corner.

"Look," she said, dangling the locket in front of Lucy's face.

"Oh, Annie!" Lucy exclaimed. "It's *weltich* (worldly)! Where did you get it?"

"I found it on the mantel in our house. Look inside."

Lucy gingerly opened the heart-shaped case and saw a familiar face. "That's your mom!" she exclaimed.

"Yes, isn't she pretty?" Annie replied. "She's wearing her going-away dress. The picture was taken on her wedding day. I'll keep it forever," she vowed.

"*Nee, du erlaabt net* (no, you aren't allowed)," Lucy said bluntly.

"But it's my mom. If you won't tell and I won't, who

would know?" Annie was nearly in tears.

"What if Mom would find it?"

"Oh, I don't think she will. I'll hide it real good. And you won't tell, Lucy, will you? I need to look at it sometimes."

"But jewelry is a sin, too, for *unser Leit* (our people)," Lucy answered hesitantly.

"If I don't wear it but only look, it won't be such a big sin, will it?" Annie asked.

"I don't know," Lucy answered. "Let's say our prayer and go to bed. *Mei Fiess sin kalt* (my feet are cold)."

"Alright, Lucy," Annie complied. As though seeking assurance, she begged once more, "You really won't tell, will you?"

Lucy had already given her word not to tell, but Annie was uneasy. A few days later, Lucy was miffed at Annie again.

"Are you finished with your homework, Annie?" Lucy asked.

School assignments were always tackled after all other tasks were completed. Supper was over and the dishes done. Annie had gone straight to her arithmetic. She worked quietly until every problem was solved.

Lucy, however, had hidden a puzzle book inside her arithmetic book. On the pretense of doing her numbers, she was playing with the puzzles.

"Yes, I'm finished," Annie told her.

"Here, then, do mine," Lucy said, shoving her book toward Annie.

"Oh, no," Annie remarked. "That would be cheating. It isn't right." She was shocked that Lucy would demand such a thing.

"What's going on?" Roman asked, hearing the commotion.

"Annie won't help me with my arithmetic," Lucy said.

"Is that true, Annie?" Dad asked.

"I'll help her, but—" She stopped.

"But what?" he prompted.

"Well, I don't like to say it," Annie squirmed.

"I want you to say it," Dad insisted.

"I'll tell you, but please don't punish her because of me," Annie tearfully requested.

"If Lucy needs punishment, it won't be because of you. Now tell me what happened."

"I finished my problems, and Lucy wanted me to do hers."

"So! And just why don't you have yours done, Lucy?" he asked his daughter.

She didn't answer.

Reaching down for her book, her dad discovered the puzzles.

"You have been playing instead of doing your work. That isn't the way we do things around here. You know that."

Roman took the puzzle book from his daughter and told her to get to work. "Never again do I want to hear of you trying something like this."

Lucy was upset with herself because she had been caught in the act. She was upset with Annie because she had refused to help her. It was Annie's fault. If Father hadn't heard Annie's expression of surprise, he wouldn't have known. Because of Annie, Lucy was scolded.

Now was the time to get even, Lucy decided. "Dad," she blurted out, "Annie has a locket."

"A what?" Roman asked. He had no idea what a locket was.

"A gold heart on a chain with her mother's picture inside," Lucy tattled.

Annie wished she had not shared her secret with Lucy. It did not make her into a friend, as she had hoped. Annie felt sick.

22
A New Home

When Roman Troyer saw the locket, he tried to make Annie understand.

"We cannot have such a worldly thing in our house," he explained. "I know it means a lot to you, but our people feel it is wrong." He spoke kindly to the tearful girl. "The Bible forbids it, and so do I. As long as you are Amish, you must abide by our teaching. I will not have it under my roof. Get rid of it."

Annie half expected Roman to toss it into the stove. But surprise of all surprises—he handed it back to her. "Now mind, you get rid of it," he told her again.

"I will," Annie promised. "I won't keep it here any longer."

She knew right away what she must do. After school she would run to the Leaning Tree and hide it in a big hole in its trunk. She didn't care if Lucy saw her run to Button Shoe Hollow. If Mr. Troyer questioned her, she could truthfully say she took it back.

Annie found an empty medicine bottle, slipped the locket inside, and screwed the cap on firmly to protect it. At the Leaning Tree, she found an old squirrel hole within reach and buried the bottle with its precious keepsake down in the rotted wood at the bottom of the cavity.

If her mother was still living, she might come back to the cottonwood tree and find it. Annie might go back once in a while to see if it was still there. She would look at it there, but not in the Troyer's house.

True to Annie's predictions, Lucy told on her. By the time Annie arrived back from the hollow, Susan knew where she had been.

"You're late," Susan said. "Lucy told me she saw you run down to Button Shoe Hollow. What did you want there?"

"I went to take the locket back," Annie replied. "Dad said he doesn't want it in this house, so I took it back. If my mom ever comes, she might find it. I put it at her Leaning Tree. That is one place she would go, for sure. Did I do right?" she asked.

"Yes, Annie, you did right. You took it back," Mrs. Troyer reassured her. "Now, girls, get your snack so you'll be ready to do chores."

Then Mom stepped into the pantry to get supplies for supper.

"You!" spat Lucy when the girls were alone. "You get away with anything! If that were me, I would have received a good scolding.

"You were told to get rid of the locket. You didn't get rid of it. I know why you put it where you did. That way you can go and get it again.

"I would have been scolded for coming home late. But not you! Oh no, not Pet Annie!"

"Oh, Lucy, don't say such things," begged Annie. "Your parents are good to you. Remember the other night when you had such a bad earache? Your mom excused you from your chores. The day you forgot your school lunch, your dad brought it to school. He made a special trip.

"What about the time you lost your second pair of gloves? They didn't scold or call you careless. Your mom told you not to worry. She could soon knit another pair.

"And I know your Mom put off buying stockings for herself so she could get material to make a warm chore *Wammes* (coat) for you," Annie reminded her.

The girls thought they were alone, eating their after-school half-moon pies. However, Mom had heard the entire conversation from the pantry because the door was ajar. She had sensed for some time the resentment her daughter felt toward Annie. The situation made her feel sad and ashamed.

"Roman," she approached her husband later that evening. "Now that the children are all in bed and the house is quiet, I have to talk with you."

"Well, talk about what?" Roman said, laying aside his *Farm Journal*. "Let's hear it."

"I'm almost ashamed to say this," Susan replied with a worried look. "It pains me to think how unkind and jealous our oldest daughter seems to be."

"Ya so, what has she done now?"

Susan repeated the conversation she had overheard earlier. Roman was shocked.

"It looks as if I will have to talk to Lucy again," he remarked. "If she could only understand that Annie needs extra help. She has lost her mother and is going through a difficult time."

A few things were coming together in Susan's mind, and she shared them with her husband. "A while ago Elva Garver told me she needs a *Kindsmaad* (baby-sitter), especially during chore time. They do a lot of milking, and it's hard to drag the little ones to the barn twice a day.

"Perhaps it would be better to separate Lucy and Annie for a while and solve Elva's problem and our problem at the same time."

"Are you thinking of sending Annie over to help?" Roman asked.

"She would still be able to go to Button Shoe School," Susan reasoned. "They need her chiefly for the morning and evening. What do you think?"

"You know better about such things than I do," Roman answered.

"We could try it if Elva Garver is willing," Susan said. "Annie is no trouble. She wants to please, and I know she loves babies. In fact, I've seen her care for Elva's youngest one after church while we women were eating."

Roman approved of Susan's plan. "Why don't you ask Elva this Sunday, then? It's our church Sunday, you know."

Elva Garver was more than willing to have Annie come and help out. "How soon can I have her?" she asked Susan.

"Well, I haven't said anything to her yet," Susan

told her. "First I wanted to see if you agree. We could bring her over tomorrow after school if she is willing. I will tell her today yet," Susan promised.

"Has she been any problem to you?" Elva inquired.

"Oh, no, she's well-behaved. There seems to be some jealousy on Lucy's part," Susan admitted with some embarrassment.

"Why don't we ask her together," Elva suggested. "She's watching my baby right now."

Annie could not believe it. Mrs. Garver wanted her to come and live with them! She would get to take care of the baby every day and watch two-year-old Katie.

"When can I go?" Annie asked.

"Tomorrow after school, if you want to," Susan answered.

"Oh, I want to!" Annie replied with excitement. She went to find Lucy.

"I'm going to have a new home, Lucy," Annie said. "Mrs. Garver wants me to live with them."

23
A Kindsmaad

Annie knew from the first day at Amos and Elva Garver's that she would like it there. Elva Garver was young and full of energy. She had a good sense of humor. This proved itself many times when things seemed to go wrong.

Elva led a disciplined life but was not easily discouraged. Her husband, Amos, was a jolly person. Strong, and a hard worker, he was respected in the Amish community and the church.

The first night Annie spent at the Garver's place, she was a bit reluctant to sleep upstairs alone. After school Elva had shown her to her room.

"We'll miss you, Annie," Susan Troyer had told her when she brought Annie's belongings over right after school. "Perhaps it's best this way. Elva needs help more than I do. After all, I have Lucy, and Bertha is learning to do more chores. We will see you at church, and the children will be at school."

"If my mom should come back—I mean, if it was a mistake . . ." Annie found it hard to express herself. "Will you tell her where I am?"

"Ach, Annie," Susan sighed. After a brief pause, she said, "Of course I would tell her. I'm sorry Lucy was so mean to you at times. I don't know what made her act that way. Maybe you were together too much. Anyway, we'll see how it works out for you to live with the Garver's for a while," Susan told her.

"Oh, I know it'll work good," Annie assured her.

Neither one knew just how long that little while might be.

Now, as Elva showed Annie where to put her clothes, Annie expressed her delight.

"This whole big room is just for me?" she asked. "No one else sleeps in here? That chest of drawers is plenty big. My clothes won't nearly fill it. The closet has way too many hooks for my dresses. And a bed-side stand with an oil lamp! Look, is this wall *Schpieggel* (mirror) for me, too?"

Elva laughed at Annie's enthusiasm and expressions. "No one else is here that can use it. Yes, Annie, this is your room. I hope you will like it here with us."

"Oh, I know I will!" Annie responded.

"I believe I hear Katie calling," Elva told Annie. "She just woke up from her nap. Finish putting your things away. I'll go on downstairs, and you come when you're finished. Take your time."

Annie looked all around the pleasant room. Everything was so neat and clean. She touched the crocheted doily on the stand. Running her fingers over the pretty lone-star quilt, she admired its colors of gold, brown, orange, and pale yellow.

Beside the lamp lay a Bible and a bookmark. Annie liked the bookmark picture of Jesus, the Good Shepherd.

"It's such a nice room," she told Elva as she came to join her.

"I'm glad you like it," Elva responded. "Do you want to feed the baby? It's time for his bottle, and I need to turn the eggs in the incubator before time to do the milking."

"I'd like to feed him," Annie agreed readily. "Sometimes after church, I hold him while you eat, and we get along fine."

"Yes, I know, and you're a good *Kindsmaad* (babysitter). I'll change him and warm the bottle. Please get the toy box out of that closet, and Katie can play while I tend the incubators."

Annie didn't know what incubators were, but it didn't matter. She started Katie playing with a string of wooden spools and some blocks.

Katie looked questioningly at Annie, knowing she was a stranger. But she did not shy away from Annie. Perhaps it was the soft tone of her voice or the smile that won Katie over. She kept watching Annie but did not cry.

"Looks like Katie is taking to you already," Elva said, handing the baby to Annie. "That's good. I wondered how she would do. I'm going down in the basement now. When the baby has taken half the milk, you need to burp him. You do know how to burp a baby, don't you?"

"Oh, yes. I often did that with Esther Troyer when

she was younger," Annie reassured her.

"If you need me, you know where I am. The basement door opens out of the pantry." With those instructions, Elva left Annie to watch the children.

"What's an incubator?" Annie asked Elva when she returned from the basement.

"It's a big wooden frame, almost like a cupboard," Elva responded. "There are trays and trays of eggs inside. It stays warm, just like under a hen, so the eggs will hatch. We use battery-operated lights for heat. Every day the trays must be pulled out and the eggs turned. The chicks hatch out after three weeks of the eggs being incubated. We'll have about three hundred chicks if nothing goes wrong."

"Yellow, fluffy, chicks?" Annie exclaimed.

"That's right."

"What's right?" Elva and Annie had not noticed Amos until he spoke.

"I was telling Annie we should have three hundred chicks soon," Elva answered.

"Don't count your chicks before they hatch, I always say," laughed Amos.

"I wasn't counting, just hoping," Elva replied.

Chore time went well. Johnny lay in his playpen while Annie played with Katie. Later she helped with supper. It was a pleasant day.

Elva went upstairs with Annie and made sure she knew how to carefully light the kerosene lamp.

"You may turn the lamp down low and burn it all night if you wish. Sleep well! Good night."

Annie was grateful. The room didn't look the same in the lamplight. A *Kindsmaad* must be brave.

24

From Kindsmaad to Regular Maad

Annie had not been gone two weeks until Lucy wished her back. She found that much of the work Annie had been doing was now required of her. Precious little time was left for play.

When she did find time, who could she play with? Her sister Bertha was too young to enjoy the things Lucy was interested in. True, she had been jealous of Annie and mistreated her. Still, Lucy remembered the fun they shared.

She thought of the many nights laughing at the strange shadow pictures they made on the wall. The dim kerosene lamp cast eerie light by which they created funny animal and people silhouettes, using their hands for different shapes. How they had giggled as they acted out the song of "Ten in a Bed."

This would often continue until her dad would call

up the stairway. *"Maed* (girls)!" he would remind them. "It's time you settle down, or I'll come up there."

Both girls knew what the consequences would be if Roman Troyer had to come upstairs. Scooting way under the covers, the girls would try to supress their giggling. Now Lucy wished with all her heart that Annie was back.

Annie, however, began to adjust well to her new home.

"Oh, Annie," Lucy approached her at school recess. "How long are you staying at the Garver place?"

"I don't know," Annie replied. "I guess as long as they need me. Why do you ask?"

"I want you to come back," Lucy said.

Annie looked surprised. "You do? I thought you didn't care to be my friend."

"Really, I do. It isn't the same anymore. Bertha sleeps with me now. She gets scared when I make shadow pictures. You can't imagine what an *unruhich* (restless) sleeper she is.

"Half the night I'm without covers. She steals them. Ask Elva Garver if she can find someone else. I'm sorry I told about your locket. If you come back, I won't be mean to you anymore."

Annie didn't know what to say. How could she believe Lucy? It takes much longer to build up trust than to tear it down.

"Lucy, I'm glad you want to be friends again," Annie finally told her. "But I cannot ask Elva Garver to let me come back to your place. She needs me, and I like helping her.

"You should see my room. It's nice and big. Sometimes it's kind of scary upstairs all alone. But then I just remember that God is with me. My real mother told me that we have guardian angels watching over us, and I should trust in God.

"I think of those things, and they help me go to sleep. There was another verse I learned when I was a little girl. I think it's in one of the psalms."

"Well, what is it?" Lucy asked.

"You, Lord, will keep me in perfect peace if my mind is fixed on you," Annie said.

"What does it mean?" Lucy questioned.

"Mother told me that if I think about the Lord when I'm anxious, he'll give me perfect peace, and then I won't be frightened."

"Oh," Lucy remarked. "I'm going to try that, too. I'll ask Mom if she will see if Elva can't get someone else to be her *Kindsmaad* (baby-sitter)."

"We ought to go and play with the other girls," Annie suggested. "Why don't you ask your mother if you can come over some Sunday afternoon? I could show you my room, and we could play then," Annie proposed.

"I'll ask her tonight," Lucy promised.

The other schoolgirls had started a game of lose your supper with the younger children.

"We wondered if you two weren't going to join us," Dena said as Lucy and Annie approached.

"You must have had something important to talk about," Christina laughed.

"Are you going to let us in on your secret, or are you going to play?" Mabel said.

"Both," Annie answered. "I want to play, and we

don't have a secret. Lucy wants me to ask Elva Garver if she can find another *Kindsmaad*. Lucy wants me back again."

Annie smiled. It was easy to see she was pleased, but yet she liked it at the Garver's. How could she leave dear little Katie and chubby, dimpled baby Johnnie? She felt torn between two decisions.

Somehow it put her mind at ease when she heard Ella Maust's remark. "Well, I suppose that will be up to Elva and Susan as to where Annie lives."

"Of course. That's the way it will be," Annie replied. Now her mind was at ease as she joined the game with her friends.

True to her word, Lucy approached her mother that very evening about having Annie back.

"Ach, I can't do that," Susan told her daughter. "Elva Garver needs her more than I do. It seemed it was not going too well with you two, so Dad and I felt it might be best to separate you."

"For how long?" Lucy asked.

"I suppose as long as Elva needs her," Susan answered.

Several weeks later on an in-between Sunday when there were no services, the Troyer's were invited for Sunday dinner at the Garver's home.

"Well, how do you like your *Kindsmaad?*" Susan asked Elva.

"Real well," Elva replied. "In fact, I have a feeling she'll stay and become my regular *Maad* (maid, hired girl). We plan to keep her."

Lucy did not like it. Not at all.

25
A Fish Tale

One after another, years came and went while Annie stayed on with the Garver family. In the six years she worked for Elva, three new babies were born to the family. Every day was a busy day.

Annie, who was now a *Yungfraa* (young lady) was a good *Maad* (maid). At age fifteen, she had completed eight grades of school. Once Amish boys and girls had passed grade eight, they were permitted to quit school and be supervised in vocational training by their parents.

What more does a boy need to work on the farm? reasoned the Amish. A young boy or girl learns more from actual experience. One does not learn how to plow straight furrows or thresh wheat in school.

How many girls learn more about caring for a baby or churning butter in school rather than working alongside their mothers? Thus, Annie was learning the importance of homemaking as she worked with Elva.

Annie had just turned seventeen and was thinking of her future.

"Elva," Annie said one day. "Do you think I will ever have a home of my own?"

"Ach, I wouldn't be surprised. Several boys have been asking to take you home from the singings, haven't they?" Elva answered.

"Yes, but I don't much care to go with them," Annie said. "I like going with Leon and Lucy. Sometimes Lucy is invited to have a ride home with someone else, so Leon brings me home. The Troyers are so nice to me."

"Abe Kinsinger brought you home several times, I thought. He seems like a nice fellow. What happened?" Elva asked. "Didn't he ask you anymore?"

"Yes, he did ask to bring me back from Sunday-night singing. He's nice, but Lucy said I was trying to steal him away from her. He had given Lucy rides several times before he asked me.

"Elva, I would never try to take him away from anyone. Now when he asks me, I say no."

"I'm afraid Lucy still has a problem with jealousy," Elva remarked. "Her mother told me of several episodes they had with her while you were there years ago. But you were youngsters then."

"I know," Annie replied. "Never once did I want her to be envious of me. She is my friend. We do have some good times visiting after church and at each other's houses.

"We are even thinking of joining church together this fall. Do you think I'm ready? I understand most of the *Pennsilfaanish Deitsch* (Pennsylvania German,

Dutch) Amish language, and I can speak it more and more. What do you think?"

Elva was taken by surprise. "Why, Annie, I didn't know you felt at home that much with *unser Leit* (our people)."

"Oh, I do," Annie assured her.

"I'm glad. You aren't joining only because Lucy is, are you?"

"No, I told Lucy first that I plan to join and be baptized. I want to live a Christian life like you and the Troyers do. Then Lucy said she wanted to join too."

"When the time comes, we will speak to the bishop," Elva said.

"Do you think he'll say yes?" Annie inquired.

"I'm sure he will," Elva told her.

That put Annie's mind at ease, and work seemed lighter.

In a household of six little ones, one never knows what to expect. Elva had to take her oldest daughter to the doctor. Katie had stepped on a rusty nail a week or so ago.

Although Elva had faithfully soaked her foot in hot Epson salt water and applied the usual salve, it got worse. During the night, Katie cried with pain. By morning, red streaks were halfway to her knee.

"I don't like the looks of this," Amos told his wife. "We've tried our home remedies. I believe it's time we have Doc Humes have a look at it. I'll hitch up Cap for you right after breakfast. Maybe it's the start of blood poisoning. I don't like it at all."

Katie, who was eight and a half years old, thought it took longer to drive the five miles to town than ever before. When they arrived at the doctor's office, there was only one other buggy tied to the hitching rail.

With the help of her mother, Katie hobbled in as well as she could. The door to the doctor's office was open, and he looked up as Elva and Katie stepped into the small waiting room.

"*Was kummt do* (what comes here)?" he asked.

The Amish people were delighted that the good doctor could speak in their dialect.

"Sit down," he invited. "I'll soon be finished here. Then I'll be right with you."

Elva saw Sylvia Witmer and her baby in the office. She heard the doctor say to Sylvia, "Mrs. Witmer, you need not worry. Your baby doesn't have measles. It's a simple case of heat rash.

"You have him dressed too warm. Young mothers are often overly anxious with the first baby, afraid they aren't keeping them warm enough. I'll give you an ointment for the rash. With that and a few less blankets, he should clear up soon."

Mrs. Witmer and Elva bid each other the time of day, and then the doctor called the Garvers into his office. He confirmed Mr. Garver's diagnosis that blood poisoning had indeed set in. After giving Katie a shot and some antibiotic pills, he said, "If this foot isn't better by tomorrow, I want to see Katie again."

While Elva was gone, Annie had her hands full. Little Viola broke the goldfish bowl, and Annie had a time of it catching the four slippery creatures.

"We'll put them in the washbasin until your mother gets home and decides what to do," she said. "They don't have much water to swim in, but it'll have to do."

Robert heard her and figured out a better place. As Annie dipped water from the stove's reservoir to clean up a spill Elsie had made, she found four dead fish floating in the hot water.

"I gave them lots of water," Robert said innocently.

"What a fish tale I will have to tell," laughed Annie.

26
The Painted Lady

Annie and Katie were weeding the garden. They had been out since right after breakfast. Now at ten o'clock, the sun was getting rather warm.

"I'm hot," Katie complained. "My back hurts and the sweat is causing my eyes to burn. Can't we stop?"

"We only have one more row after this," Annie said. "I know you're hot and tired. If you help me finish weeding without grumbling, we'll wade in the lake to cool off," Annie promised.

"Really?" Katie wanted to be sure.

"Yes, really. You begin at one end of the row. I'll take the other end, and we'll meet in the middle."

"Annie, I like you for a *Maad*," Katie told her. "You know how to make work seem like fun sometimes."

"It's better to think about the rest you have coming after work than how hard and endless the job is," Annie replied.

How refreshing the cool lake water felt as it swirled

around the girls' bare feet and legs. They did not dare raise their dresses above the knees. That would be immodest.

Little minnows darted around their feet. Katie tried to catch one, but they were too quick. A black-and-yellow mottled butterfly flitted from branch to branch among a bed of cattails. A yellow finch swung from a nearby thistle stalk.

The sky was so blue. It was a perfect summer day.

"We'd better go in now and help your mom," Annie said.

"*Ach, fer was misse mir immer schaffe* (oh, why do we always have to work)?" Katie lamented.

"The Bible says that the one who does not work shall not eat," Annie replied.

"I don't mind working some of the time, but not *all* the time," Katie told her.

"Come on, let's go."

Reluctantly Katie obeyed. The two girls had enjoyed their short excursion in the lake so much that they had not noticed a car turning in the drive.

"Look!" exclaimed Katie. "I bet we have company."

As they approached the house, they were surprised to see a stylish lady. She turned as she heard footsteps on the walk.

"Hello," she said. "I knocked several times, but no one answered. A baby was crying somewhere inside, so I suppose no one heard my knock. Do you live here?"

"Well, she does," Annie told her, pointing to Katie. "I just work here."

"Well, I'm looking for a girl by the name of Pearlie

Mae Streeter," the lady informed them. "I was told she lives among your people. Can you tell me if you have heard of her?"

Annie began to tremble all over.

"Why are you looking for her?" she asked in a voice unlike her own.

"I'm her Aunt Myrtle, and I heard her mother died. If that's true, maybe she can tell me what happened."

Annie finally spoke. "I was Pearlie Mae, but now I'm Annie.

"No," the lady replied, "you can't be my niece. Why, you don't look at all like Pearlie Mae."

"But I am. You don't recognize me because I look different now—I'm Amish."

The lady laughed and said, "If you're Pearlie Mae, prove it. Where did you live when you were a little girl?"

"We lived in Button Shoe Hollow in the cabin," Annie told her.

"What did your mother look like, and why did she put you with these people?" Myrtle questioned further.

"She didn't put me with the family where I'm working now. First I lived with the Troyer family. When Elva, who lives here, needed a baby-sitter, they took me. Now I'm their *Maad*—I mean, hired girl.

"It's been six years since I came here. Let me ask Mrs. Garver if I can take you to the cabin. I want to show you something to prove that I was Pearlie Mae."

Elva was as shocked as Annie at this unexpected event. She had been busy in the back part of the house and failed to hear Myrtle's knocking.

"*Was in die Welt selle mir duh* (what in the world shall we do)?" she asked, and then added with a worried look, "Did she come to get you?"

"I don't know, but I'm not going with her if she did," Annie declared. "She doesn't believe I am Pearlie Mae. Is it alright if I take her to the cabin so I can prove it?

"The locket with my mother's picture is there. When she sees that, she'll *have* to believe me. Long ago I hid it in my Leaning Tree, because Mr. Troyer said such things are worldly. I'll come right back," Annie promised.

"Take Katie with you then, and don't stay long," Elva advised.

Katie was awed by the big, shiny car and the gaudy woman. She kept staring at her long, painted nails and green eye shadow. After slowly walking to the car, Katie whispered to Annie, "What does the painted lady want, and where are we going?"

Annie explained as well as she could.

When they reached the large cottonwood, Annie dug deep inside the cavity until her fingers found the medicine bottle with the locket inside. She took the cap off the bottle and shook the cool object into her hand.

"Here," she said, handing the locket to Myrtle. "Open it."

"Sure enough!" she exclaimed immediately. "It *is* my sister. But, Pearlie, how you've changed! Do you like being Amish?"

"Yes, I like it, and I'm going to join their church soon," Annie informed her. "I'd never go back anywhere else. The Amish are my people now."

"Well, it beats me how anyone can be so quaint and be satisfied with that kind of life. Tell me what happened to your parents," Myrtle insisted.

Annie told her about Uncle Louie's letter, and that that was all she knew.

"You may have the locket, Aunt Myrtle," Annie offered. "It's too worldly for us Amish, and my mom is your sister."

Myrtle took the girls back to the house and gave Annie a warm good-bye.

As she left, Katie told Annie she was glad the painted lady didn't make Annie go with her.

So was Annie.

27

Unexpected Events

"Elva," said Amos Garver, "do you think you still need a *Maad*? Katie is old enough to do a fair share of work. Seems to me she depends on Annie too much."

"Ya, Amos," Elva agreed. "I've noticed that, too. But Annie has been here over six years. She seems like one of the family. She is such a good worker."

"*Ich weess* (I know), but Elsie can take on some of Katie's duties. It costs to have a full-time hired girl. By spring I'll need a part-time hired hand for the farm-work. You know we can't afford both. I think you had better let Annie look for another place."

"Ya, I will," Elva consented. "It won't be easy. Where would she go?"

"Don't worry," Amos reassured her. "Annie will find a place. Our women are always needing help."

Elva knew this was true. Some families needed help preparing for church services to be held at their house. New *Buppelin* (babies) were making their arrivals, or school sewing took up extra time. Gardening and canning were extra tasks.

Many of these were short jobs consisting of two to four weeks. This was difficult for a *Maad*. She had to learn where kitchen utensils, pots, and pans were kept in each house. Each housewife had a different way of operating her household.

About the time a *Maad* learned the routine and was accepted by the little ones, it was time to move on. Most Amish women were easy to work for, but a few were not.

That Saturday evening, Annie had just finished washing her hair. It hung in soft beautiful waves around her face.

As she walked through the kitchen, Elva said, "Before you go to bed, I want to talk with you, Annie."

"Well, I'll have to let my hair dry anyway, so I'm going to be up a while longer."

"Come, sit here by me," Elva invited.

Annie detected a note of sadness in her voice. "What is it?" she asked. "Elva, have I done something wrong?"

"No, not at all. I must tell you something I wish I wouldn't need to say. You're a good *Maad* and have helped me for a long time. You seem like family to me. But Amos thinks I no longer need a *Maad*. He says Katie and Elsie are old enough to help more. Ach, Annie, I wish you could stay."

Annie was stunned. After over six years, she assumed this would be her home. It was so sudden. At first, she was too choked up to speak.

"I'm sorry," Elva said. "Amos says he needs a part-time hired man. We would need your room for him."

"I understand." Annie answered. She turned her face away to hide her disappointment.

"Tomorrow is our church Sunday," Elva continued. "I'm sure someone will be looking for a *Maad*." She was feebly trying to soften the blow.

"I'll ask around," Annie answered. Somehow she wished Elva would have waited to tell her until Monday. At least she would have had a busy day to help work through this news.

Annie went to bed. She tossed and turned. Would she be able to go on with her plans of joining the church? Perhaps where she would be working would be too far for Leon Troyer to take her along to singings or other youth gatherings. Would she ever have a place she could call home?

Creeping softly across the room, Annie stood by the window. Gazing out into the night, she thought of her past. It all seemed so long ago. She had learned to love the way of the Amish people. She was well liked by young and old alike, and she truly felt as one of them. But now! Where, oh, where would she go?

She wondered if she should have gone with her Aunt Myrtle. Her aunt had not asked her to go with her. Annie knew she would not have felt comfortable with the painted lady anyway. She was surprised that Aunt Myrtle came at all.

While her aunt talked with Annie, she told her what a terrible father she had.

"I always told your mother not to marry that no-good bum! She wouldn't listen. I knew he'd end up in prison."

Annie resented such talk. She had told Myrtle to stop it. "When my dad was not drinking, he was good to us. Mama said it was a sickness."

"Precious few times he wasn't drinking," Aunt Myrtle had smirked. "Sickness indeed! Call it what you will. Boy, if he could see you now!" Myrtle laughed.

The conversation kept haunting Annie. She wanted to forget it.

A dog barked in the distance, and an owl hooted from a nearby tree, drawing Annie's thoughts back to the present. Shivering, she stole back to her bed. She pulled the covers around her and began silently to pray.

Annie asked the Lord to quiet her troubled heart. The answer came to her mind so plainly that she could not ignore it. As though borne on the whispering wind, words from Scripture touched her soul: "Be still and know that I am God."

So also she remembered, "Whenever I am afraid, I will trust in you, Lord." That was all she needed to do. Trust and wait.

Annie slept.

Before the next day was through, Annie had a new *Maad* job. A mother with a set of four-year-old twins and a two-year-old boy was having another child in a few weeks. She was desperately looking for a *Maad*.

Although Annie's friends told her it was a hard place to work, she let Mrs. Bowman know she would come. That night Leon picked her up as usual for singing. She told him about her move.

"Oh, Leon, you need not take me to the singings

anymore," she told him. "It's out of your way.

"Ach, I wonder if I'll ever have a home of my own. You're such a kind friend, Leon, but you need not take me along anymore."

"I had thought maybe we could be more than just friends," Leon said. "You'll have a home alright, if I can help it."

Annie was startled. What did Leon mean?

28
Difficult Situations

Monday morning came too soon for Annie. She didn't like good-byes. Elva and the children tried to act cheerful to keep Annie's spirits up. It was no use. They could not hide their true feelings.

"I don't want you to go," Katie told Annie as she watched her gather her things and pack a suitcase.

"I know," Annie responded. "Maybe it's best this way, though. In the six-plus years I've been here, I let myself get close to you all. It seems like I belong to the family—but I don't. Katie, *I don't belong anywhere!*

"Do you know how that feels? Of course you don't. You have a mother and father, brothers and sisters, and you . . ." Annie stopped.

"Now I must not feel sorry for myself. Guess I'll move on wherever I'm needed. The Lord will lead me because I asked him to." Annie buckled her suitcase straps, gave her cargo a final check, and started downstairs with her load.

"Will you bring my handbag and Sunday shoes?" Annie asked Katie.

Katie picked up those articles and solemnly followed. Mr. Bowman was already waiting to take Annie to her new job.

"Here, I'll carry that for you," he said as he reached for Annie's suitcase. "My land, it's heavy. What you got in here, *goldnich Bacheschtee* (gold bricks)?" he teased.

In spite of her sadness, Annie smiled. The thought of her having even *one* gold brick seemed ridiculous. She had heard that Eli Bowman was a jolly good-natured man. However, his wife, Lizzie, had an entirely opposite reputation.

"Come back and see us whenever you can," Elva told Annie.

"I'll try, but I have no transportation," she replied.

"That's no problem," Elva assured her. "Let us know when you can come. We'll see that you get here."

They shook hands as they parted. Annie did not trust herself to look back.

Eli clicked to his horse, and they were on their way, carrying many memories along for Annie.

She saw the two little faces as soon as she opened the front gate. Precious faces of two little boys, their noses pressed against the windowpane. Curious eyes shone up at her in expectation.

"Hello," Annie said, smiling at their sweet expressions.

"Well, what took you so long getting here?" Lizzie Bowman asked as she came into the kitchen.

Without waiting for an answer, she made her own

assumptions. "Eli had to talk all morning with Amos Garver, that's what. Then they say us women gossip. Huh! Well, get a move on, Annie. Take your things upstairs.

"The room at the head of the stairs to the left is where you'll sleep. Set your things in there. You can put them away before you go to bed tonight.

"Samuel and Daniel, get away from that window," Lizzie scolded. "You have them all marked up again. Just because you see your daddy out there, you needn't go funny. Get away, I said."

Annie saw them cringe as Lizzie took each by the arm and jerked them across the room. "Now sit here and don't move until I say you can."

Then she looked at Annie, who was staring in unbelief at what she saw and heard. "What are you waiting for?" Lizzie snapped. "Didn't I tell you to take your things upstairs? Get to it!"

Annie snatched up her belongings and carried them to the small, drab room which would be her prison for a month. She dreaded telling Lizzie Bowman about her laundry that needed to be washed.

"You dirtied them while working for the Garvers," Mrs. Bowman informed her. "That is where they should have been done. Well, you might as well add them to ours."

The four-year-old twins and two-and-a-half-year-old Freddie loved their father. Sometimes Annie thought Lizzie was jealous of the boys' preference for Eli. But she did nothing to increase their affection for her.

Annie's friends were right; Mrs. Bowman was hard

to please. She had a sharp tongue and a sour disposition.

One day when the twins tracked mud into the house, Lizzie told Annie, "I hope this next baby is a girl. With three boys, Eli will have all the help, once they're grown. You would think I'd deserve something good."

Annie had to wonder if she didn't care for her boys at all. Lizzie did seem more lenient with Freddie.

True to his word, Leon Troyer continued taking Annie to youth gatherings, even when he had to drive far out of his way. She often wondered what he meant by his earlier remark of being more than a friend. He never mentioned it again, and she did not question him.

Annie could confide in Leon and did so many times. She told him how Lizzie Bowman scolded her twins for putting fingerprints on the windowpanes.

"I once read a poem about a mother who scolded her child for the same thing," she told him. "Later on, the child died, and then how the mother wished for fingerprints on the panes. It made me cry when I read it."

Annie worked for many families after she left the Bowman's place. Yes, Lizzie had a beautiful baby girl. For the first time, she seemed to be in a generally pleasant mood.

Other boys would often offer Annie a ride home from youth activities or singings. When she accepted, Leon would become quiet and even withdrawn.

Annie was now a member in the Amish church. She would be twenty-one on her next birthday. Lucy

Troyer had asked her forgiveness long ago. Annie spent most of her free weekends at Roman Troyer's place. This still seemed more like family to her. Lucy was keeping company with Abe Kinsinger.

"Annie," Lucy said one evening, "you have let Melvin Fry take you home from the last three singings. Are you two getting serious?"

"No," laughed Annie.

"Well, I'm glad," Lucy said, "because Leon is going to ask you to go steady."

"*Du mehnst net* (you don't mean it)!" Annie exclaimed.

"Yes, I do. He told me secretly. Don't let on you know. But when he asks, what will you say?"

"What should I say?"

"That's for you to figure out. But now you have time to think it over."

The girls giggled, excited about life unfolding before them.

29
The Right Choice

Life held so many decisions for Annie. Mrs. Bowman needed a *Maad* again. She was laid up with a badly broken ankle. Annie happened to finish up a baby-case job and needed to find employment soon.

When Lizzie Bowman sent word inquiring if she was available, Annie didn't know what to say. She dreaded the thought of working for this woman again. But what choice did she have? Annie felt she would be imposing on the Troyer's by asking to stay there.

She needed to lay aside money, for she had no home. Annie did not want charity. She was determined that with God's help, she would earn her own way.

Therefore, she went back to work for the Bowmans once more. To her surprise, she found Lizzie quite pleasant. The twins were nine years old and a big help. Freddie was a lively seven-year-old, and little Susie was a joy. Annie was glad she came back.

Sunday after services, Lucy and Annie were in the washhouse at the same time. Lucy told Annie that Leon wanted her to ask if he might take her to singing that evening.

"What shall I say, Lucy?" Annie asked. "Leon seems more like a brother to me."

"Well, yes, that's right. You've lived with us so much that you are like family to us, and we're your family. And yes, we're brothers and sisters in the family of God, as the bishop says. But Leon isn't your biological brother," Lucy reminded her, "so nothing stands in the way of you two going together. He really thinks a lot of you."

"Do you think he'll ask me?" Annie inquired.

"Ask you what?" Lucy feigned innocence. She knew very well what Annie meant.

"About going steady," Annie answered.

Going steady meant a boy and a girl were keeping company with no one else. It often led to an engagement.

"I'm sure Leon will ask you," Lucy quickly assured her.

"Ach, Lucy, what shall I say? We're just friends."

"Isn't that the way all courtships start?" Lucy replied. "Abe Kinsinger and I are friends, too. Even after two people get married, they are friends—in fact, best friends."

"You're so smart, Lucy," Annie remarked. "But how did you figure that out?"

"I didn't figure it out by myself, Annie. At my great-grandmother's funeral, the bishop said it. When he preached, he shared what great-grandpa revealed to him. Great-grandpa Troyer said, '*Mei Frau waar mei beschte Freind* (my wife was my best friend).' The bishop said that's the way God meant for it to be, a married pair as best friends."

"That's beautiful," Annie replied. "Leon is a very good friend. I must think about it."

"What shall I tell him? Will you go with him tonight? You'd better give me your answer. Some of the other girls will be asking why we stayed in the washhouse so long and what we were talking about."

"Tell Leon he can take me to the singing and home afterward," Annie answered. She hoped she had made the right choice.

As they started out for the singing, Leon said, "I was surprised to hear that you are working for the Bowmans again. You must be a glutton for punishment," he joked.

"You wouldn't believe how different it is this time," Annie replied. "I actually like it there now. Lizzie Bowman seems like a new woman. She's so much kinder to her husband, and she's patient with the children.

"If I would have had another job waiting for me, I probably would have refused her. But now I'm glad I came."

"It is good when a person changes for the better," Leon agreed. "Lucy used to be so unkind to you, but now you two stick together like glue." Leon laughed comfortably.

"Lucy didn't like sharing her mother, and I can't blame her. She even had to give up some of her dresses for me. I really didn't belong there, and I know I was so different."

"You are not so different anymore," Leon assured her.

As usual, they enjoyed the singing of the sacred hymns and the fellowship. Afterward, Roy Stutzman asked Annie if he could take her home.

"I already have a ride," she politely informed him.

"Well then, what about going with me to the box social on Thursday night?" Roy asked hopefully.

Another choice to make. So many decisions were not easy. Somehow Annie found herself refusing this invitation also.

The ride home was a pleasant one. The full moon gave a twilight effect to the night.

"Annie, I would like it if you would be my steady girl," Leon said.

She knew he would ask her, but it had not been settled in her mind yet. They rode on in silence until Leon spoke again.

"Well, aren't you going to say anything? Will you be my steady?"

Annie sighed softly. In a voice scarcely above a whisper, she replied, "Yes, Leon, if you want me to, I will."

Soon it became common knowledge among the Amish that Leon Troyer and Annie Streeter were paired off, as they put it. The other fellows no longer asked for Annie's company.

Another choice had been made, and before long Annie knew it was the right one.

Leon was very happy. Many times when he came for Annie, he was whistling. One evening as he came to the Bowman's home, little Susie was on the porch.

She watched him as he came whistling up the walk.

Naturally, a person's mouth forms into a small, round shape to produce the sounds. Susie never said a word, not even when Leon stopped whistling and spoke to her. The next morning she approached Annie with a question, much to Annie's amusement.

"Why do you go with that man who swallowed his mouth, all except one little hole?" she asked.

"What?" Annie laughed. "What man?"

"The man you went with last night. He came up the walk and was going like this." Susie tried to imitate Leon.

"Ach, Susie," Annie replied. "That's my friend Leon. He didn't swallow his mouth. He was whistling because he's happy."

She could hardly wait until she could tell Leon! Annie knew he would have a good laugh.

30

A Home for Annie

Two years had passed since Leon had asked Annie to be his special friend. Now he was ready to ask her another question.

Annie had learned much of the Troyer family history. At Sunday afternoon visits and family reunions, she heard about Jake Maust and Ellie's People. Everyone in the Amish community spoke with high regard and respect concerning Leon's ancestors. Many traditions and teachings of the dear old folks were still upheld.

Annie had learned to speak Pennsylvania Dutch well. She was learning to read her German Bible, a gift from Leon. No one could honestly find fault with her housekeeping. She was a neat, attractive young woman.

Leon reflected upon these qualities. Yes, she would be a good wife. He knew of a small farm for sale that was to his liking. With his earnings from three years of working as a hired hand, he could handle the down payment. They would work hard and together, with God's help, they'd pay the farm off.

Leon had it all planned. He would tell his parents first.

Roman and Susan were pleased. "Annie has almost been like family, and now she will be," Susan told her son.

"I haven't asked her yet," Leon said.

"What if she says no?" Roman teased.

"We'll have to wait and see," Leon answered.

"Remember, Annie's first eight years of upbringing were quite different from yours," his father reminded him.

"If Annie isn't satisfied with the Amish way, it would have shown up long ago," Leon reasoned.

"That's true," Susan agreed. "I think she has proved her faithfulness."

So it came to be that Leon asked Annie to be his wife.

"You mean you want us to share our life together forever?" Annie asked. "Do you really want me? I never did belong to a family after my mom died."

"We belong together, Annie, and we'll be family."

Annie smiled. "Yes, I'll marry you."

Leon's cup of gladness overflowed. "Would this winter be too soon for you?" he asked.

"Whenever you say," Annie answered.

"How would November suit you? I am buying a small farm and would like to fix a few things up before spring fieldwork starts."

"November would be good," Annie told him. Suddenly she became quiet.

"What's wrong?" Leon asked.

"There is just one thing," she replied. "Would you take me back to Button Shoe Hollow one more time? I need to go to the Leaning Tree and lift my eyes to those hills, like my mom used to do. I'm scared, and I need to feel the peace God gave me there when I was a child."

"Why are you scared?" Leon asked.

"Because maybe I won't know how to be a good Amish *Frau* (woman of the house)," she told him.

"You are a good Amish *Maad*. It's the same, only you will be doing all the work for me," Leon teased her.

"Please, Leon, I want to go, just once," Annie requested. "If you take me now, I won't ask again. I know I can find peace wherever the Lord is, but that was a special place. My mother and I went there many times.

"Maybe it's only a way of saying good-bye to my early childhood memories, so I can put the troubled times in their proper place. Mother was a Christian and a good Mom. She would be happy to know that I will be getting such a fine husband.

"You'll take me, won't you? Please?" Annie pleaded.

How could Leon deny her request? Although he could not fully understand Annie's wish, he promised to take her. Annie brightened at his reply.

"What day in November do you think we should choose?" Annie asked. "Are we getting married at regular church services, like widower Sam Mullet and his wife did? I don't have a family to set up a regular wedding for us," she reminded Leon.

"No, but I do," he told her. "My mother assured me of that when I told them I was going to ask you to marry me. She started planning right away."

Now it was Annie's turn to tease. "And what if I would have said no?" she asked.

"In that case, I would not have been the only disappointed one," Leon remarked. "What do you say to November the first? That falls on a Thursday. The women like that day of the week. It gives them three days to prepare and two for cleanup."

It was decided; that would be the date. When Elva Garver found out that Annie was to be married, she insisted that the ceremony be at their house. Annie needed time off from *Maad* duties, so Elva invited her to spend all of October at her home. Annie was grateful.

She helped Elva with housework in exchange for late tomatoes, apples, pears, and lima beans to can. Lucy Troyer made a beautiful quilt and invited all Annie's girlfriends to help quilt. Annie sewed her own wedding dress. She was very busy, for she also helped Susan Troyer, who was determined to serve the wedding meals. There was to be a lunch, dinner, and midnight feast.

Leon did not forget. One beautiful fall day, he took Annie to Button Shoe Hollow. He remained seated in the buggy as Annie made her way through the tall grass until she reached the big cottonwood. This must be Annie's own private time. Not for one moment did Leon think of invading that sacred rendezvous.

The sky was an azure blue with fleecy white clouds

floating gently by. Annie looked beyond the hills. As the leaves of the old tree whispered softly, she made her farewell and returned to the buggy.

Leon sat with his head bowed until Annie spoke.

"Oh, Leon, it's all gone!" she exclaimed. "The cabin has been torn down, and even the old hand pump is missing. It's not the same. Maybe it's best this way. The ties are not so hard to break."

"Ya, it's the best," Leon replied.

Annie climbed to the seat beside him. "Let's go," she said. "We'll look ahead now and live one day at a time."

Annie had saved a tidy sum of money from her work as a *Maad*. What fun she had shopping and furnishing a home of her own. She was happier than she had ever been and thankful that God had led her to the Amish faith.

All the relatives included her in the lineage of Ellie's People. At last Annie had a home.